THE EPHEMERAL FILE

AN ADAM FRALEY MYSTERY

HENRY HOFFMAN

The Ephemeral File
Copyright © 2018 by Henry Hoffman

ISBN: 978-1-68046-667-6

Melange Books, LLC
White Bear Lake, MN 55110
www.melange-books.com

Published in the United States of America.

Cover Design by Fantasia Frog Designs

ACKNOWLEDGMENTS

My gratitude goes to Barbara Whelehan for her assistance in the preparation of the manuscript.

Sometimes you just have to wait for fate to make its move.

ANONYMOUS

CHAPTER ONE

May, 1995

As a matter of policy made clear from the start, the do-me-a-favor case was one Adam Fraley went to great lengths to avoid, except in this instance. The request came from Tamra Fugit, his office manager.

"He's a longtime member of my aunt's church, Adam," she explained from across his desk. She had moved from her side of the office to his, side-saddling into a chair, to underscore the personal nature of the request. "I know it's something we studiously avoid, but she's my only living relative and has done so much for me over the years."

Adam looked at her with pain in his eyes.

She crossed a leg over a well-turned knee, smoothed her reddish-brown dress-the color of her hair-and clasped her hands in her lap. "After five years on the job, I'm entitled to ask for one favor, am I not," she asked coyly.

Adam leaned back in his black leather chair and exhaled a deep breath. "What's the fellow's name?" he asked, displaying the first crack in his resolve.

"Roland Westwood. He's an elderly man who, according to my aunt, is nearing his final approach."

"How old?"

"Plus-side of seventy."

"Retired?"

"Yes. From what I understand, he spent a career in golf course management."

"What's his problem?"

"It has to do with a woman in his past," she said, as if reluctant to reveal more.

"Don't all of our problems have to do with women in our past?" Adam cracked, drawing a disgruntled look. "Can you be more specific?"

The cast of his office manager's comely face took on a more serious tone "It has to do with an old girlfriend of his. I believe she was his first date."

"First love or first date?"

"Both, from the way she explained it."

"He would like me to find her…is that it?"

"Apparently so," she said, reaching behind her head with both hands to tighten a high ponytail.

"For what reason?"

Her hair back in place, Tamra released her hands from behind her head and gave a slight shrug.

"This is sounding very much like a guy looking to find a long-lost love."

Again, she shrugged her shoulders in response. "It might be best if he gave you the details. I'm really not privy to them."

Adam cast a sour look his office manager's way. His instinct was to stick to company policy and turn thumbs down on the request. He had far better things to do than take a trip down memory lane with a septuagenarian obsessed with a first love. Still, he could plainly see those big green eyes of hers from across his desk asking the legitimate question, "Do I need to mention how many favors I have performed for you?" No, he was not about to win this exchange nor was it worth going to the mat over.

"Okay, for your aunt and for the preservation of office harmony, set up an appointment with Mr. Westwood."

"I already have," she said through a sly smile.

———

Roland Westwood was a frail man who walked with a cane. That was Adam's first impression of the man sitting across from him. His second was that he was a well-mannered individual who projected a seasoned dignity. Nonetheless, his starched blue shirt, creased tan slacks, and brown suede loafers masked a body at war with the ravages of old age. From beneath the Tampa Bay Bucs cap he was wearing flowed strands of yellowing gray hair to the nape of his neck, perhaps from all his traipsing around golf courses, Adam surmised. Nor was the Florida sun any kinder to his deeply lined, tanned face, drawn tight by sunken cheeks. Nonetheless, amid the general ebb gleamed clear blue eyes, at once alert and engaging.

"Call me Roland," he said in a raspy voice.

"Okay, Roland, what can I do for you?"

Roland nodded his head, acknowledging the invitation to carry on. "Do you remember your first date, Mr. Fraley?" he asked.

"As I recall, it was not that all memorable," he replied. "Is that what this is all about? And, please, call me Adam."

"Perhaps, if I told you a quick story, it would help explain things," he said, removing his cap and placing it on the edge of Adam's desk, revealing more yellowed hair.

"I am seventy-three years old," he began. "My story goes back almost fifty-two of those years to 1943. I was a junior student at Chapel College, a small Catholic all-male school over in eastern Pasco County near San Antonio, Florida. Are you familiar with the school and the area?"

"Somewhat...yes."

"It was a very unsettled time for me as I suppose it is for most college kids straining to make it to adulthood," he said. "The problem for me was that I didn't know what to do with my life. I had no vocation to spur me on and as a result my grades suffered. And hanging over everything was the war and the likelihood I would be drafted. Selective Service was in full operation and I was classified 1-A."

"No student deferment?" Adam asked.

"Student deferments were ended, which added to my angst," he said. "To top it all off, my social life was non-existent. I was twenty-one years old and had never had a date. I attributed that to my Catholic upbringing. Attending an all-male high school and all-male college can put a damper on social life, especially in those days when kids did not have cars of their own to hop around in. My situation was not all that unique among students. Sure, the parents could shuffle you around, but the chaperon option was never an appealing one."

Roland paused, as if expecting a reaction from Adam to his social predicament.

"Sometimes studies and the opposite sex can both be a distraction, not to mention a war going on," Adam lamely noted.

"Anyway, to escape reality, on Sunday afternoons I would sometimes trek into town to this local movie theater to catch a film. Little did I know it would lead to my first love."

We've gone from first date to first love in record time, Adam mused. *I should have assigned this case to Tamra. That's what I should have done.*

"There was this girl who worked in the theater's ticket booth who I immediately developed a big crush on. She attended a local Catholic high school and was a cheerleader. This I knew because she would wear her cheerleader's uniform to work on game days. Believe me, she was beyond beautiful and undoubtedly out of my league. The truth was the mere exchange of pleasantries with her while I was getting a ticket provided a much greater escape from my problems than the film itself."

What a sweet story, he could hear his office manager thinking from across the room as she pretended to toil away on her computer.

"Like I said, she was out of my league. I'd often see her out on the town, usually accompanied by the same fellow, a handsome guy who I later learned was the captain of the football team. Nevertheless, I was a guy at the time who had nothing to lose, so why not give it a shot and ask her out?"

"What had been her attitude toward you?" Adam asked. "Any signs of affection?"

"Small ones...enough to signal she didn't dislike me. For instance, when there was a line at the ticket window, she'd often glance back to check how long the line was. If I happened to be one of those waiting and her eye caught mine she'd react with a friendly smile, a sign she viewed me favorably, I'd concluded. Women don't smile at guys they don't like. Right?"

"Not as a rule," Adam said, acknowledging the obvious.

"So, there came a day when I was the only one in line, at which time I summoned up the courage to ask for her phone number, fully expecting her to say, 'I'm sorry, I'm seeing someone.' There was also that college versus high school guy thing at play. There was only three years difference in our ages, but the small town social mores of the time made it appear much greater.

"Anyway, what followed was the longest three seconds of my life," he continued. "I felt like stooping down to hide from her view but held my position. At first, a nearly invisible smile formed on her face. Whether it was one of surprise or expectation, I did not know. Whichever, she said nothing. Instead, she reached across from her and snatched a slip of paper, scribbled down her number, and slipped it through the ticket window to me. Needless to say, I was ecstatic."

Sitting and listening, Adam again pondered why he hadn't assigned this case to Tamra, given her vested interest in it. On second thought, it might not have been such a good idea for the very same reason.

"To make a long story short," Westwood went on, "We dated for a while, though the relationship was short lived. I was nearing the end of my junior year, which meant I would be returning to Tampa for the summer."

"You were boarding there?" Adam interjected.

"Yes, and she was one of the so-called 'town girls' who resided there with her parents. I know it's only thirty-five miles or so from here to there, but you have to realize this was back in the early forties when kids did not have cars. It might as well have been five-hundred miles. The dates I had with her were the walking type—treks to the local park or trail hikes through the woods."

"That was the end of it?" Adam asked.

"Yes. As I said, my grades were sub-par and I was still at a loss regarding my direction in life. If I was to have a future with her, I would first have to carve out a future for me...something to offer her other than youthful passion. So, I made the decision to join the Army. The war was raging with no end in sight and it was only a matter of time before I was called up anyway."

"How did she take it?"

"I had discussed it over the phone with her after I had returned home to Tampa, so it came as no big surprise. She understood my situation."

"No breaking of her heart?"

"Oh, maybe a chip but not a break. It wasn't as though she had given up everything dear to her for me. She was forthright in telling me she would be dating others."

"So, you joined the Army. Then what?"

"Then I caught a bad break. The first day at boot camp..."

"Camp Blanding?" Adam asked.

"Yes, right outside Jacksonville. As I started to say, the first day our drill instructor informs us we can make one call to our parents to let them know we made it there in one piece and that's it. To put an explanatory point on it, there were no phones in our barracks. The calls to our parents were made from a battery of phone booths outside a post recreational facility. For the remainder of our time there we would be in effect cut off from the outside world, meaning I would be out of touch with them and Staci."

"Staci was her name?"

"Yes—Staci Carew."

"No letters between you two?"

Westwood shook his head. "That's where I really screwed up. Believe it or not, I didn't have her street address. I had always met her in the morning at the theater when she had the day off. From there we would walk to wherever we were headed. Everything in that small community, the park, the nature trails, the river, was nearby. I had her phone number but that was it."

"You never met her parents?"

"Yes, one time. We walked to her house on our first date, so she could introduce me. I paid no attention to the street address. It was the last thing on my mind."

"Not a good way to keep up with the competition," Adam remarked. "No mutual friend you could contact by mail?"

"No. I could have attempted extraordinary measures, like sending a letter in care of the school but figured it would be better to bide my time and wait till boot camp was over, at which time I would be allowed a week's leave. I had told her the first thing I would do when I arrived home was to come see her. My plan was to borrow my folk's car to make the trip."

"You weren't going to call her first?"

"No, I was planning on surprising her with an in-person visit."

Westwood paused in his account to take a deep breath. "Well, the surprise ended up being on me. I arrived home on a Saturday evening and decided to drive to San Antonio immediately following Sunday morning Mass. That was my plan but, lo and behold, who do I see at the service, none other than Staci and the football captain sitting together in the front of the church. My heart sunk like a stone. The two of them attending church together in Tampa meant only one thing in my mind. They had taken the next step. They had married and settled in the city. After church I sat in my car and contemplated the coincidence of my attending the same service at the same church they had chosen to attend. I came to the conclusion it was a message sent to me by God, minus the thunder and lightning," he added with a chuckle.

"And what was the message?"

"To get on with my life. So, I did."

"So, now you want to locate her?"

"Yes, if she's still with us."

"Why?" Adam asked directly.

"I don't say this to elicit sympathy but I'm in a losing battle with cancer. According to my doctor, I have at best six months to live. As I look back over my life, I consider that brief time I spent with Staci as a turning point in my life, not to mention a missed opportunity. Yes, she is a lost love, the one I let get away."

"You never married?"

"Correct. I never married."

"You still haven't given a reason you want to get back in touch with her. I know memories are said to be the lifeblood of the elderly, but a good memory can be an argument against it. These sorts of lost-love pursuits often do not end well. There's always the risk the good memories will be shattered in the attempt to relive them, no matter how noble the intention."

"Absolutely true," he said. "Nonetheless, by not trying to reconnect with her following my enlistment, I sent a message that I didn't care about our relationship when in fact I cared deeply. If there is one matter I wish to correct before I leave this earth, it is that."

Adam studied his face for a moment before reaching for a pen and paper. "Okay, I'll need some basic info. What was her name again?"

"Staci Carew."

"You have no idea where she lives now, or if in fact, she is still living?"

"No. She could be living anywhere in the world for all I know."

"Do you have pictures of her or members of her family?"

"No."

"Any friends of hers still around?"

"I don't know. I never really got to know any of her friends."

"The name of the school she attended?"

"St. Scholastica. It was a local Catholic girls' school. It was a companion school to Highland Hills Academy, the Catholic boys' school. I believe the two merged some years back and is now called Highland Hills Prep Academy."

"Anything else?" Adam asked.

"Sorry, that's it."

"There is one question I need to ask you up front, Roland. There are no nefarious reasons for you wanting to find her. Correct?"

"Do I look like someone who could carry out nefarious acts?" Westwood answered with another chuckle, his shoulders bobbing up and down.

"As a matter of fact, looks or age have nothing to do with nefarious acts," Adam pointedly said, draining the mirth from Westwood's response.

"One more question," Adam continued. "There are outfits that specialize in these sorts of searches. Have you checked with any of them? It is becoming quite a cottage industry what with the advances in automated information retrieval and the general availability of public records. We, on the other hand, have been divorcing ourselves from this sort of case."

"You came personally recommended" he replied directly, reminding Adam of his office manager's connection to the case.

"You have not made any efforts to locate her? I do not want to be wasting my time covering ground already tracked."

"I have made no significant effort other than a couple of phone calls that led nowhere."

"Calls to whom?"

"Directory assistance. The operators said there were no listings for the name in Pasco County." Westwood shifted to a more comfortable position in his chair. "It's not that I didn't wish to conduct a search on my own. It's that I'm not physically capable. I wanted someone who could do the necessary leg work, a professional, so I came to you based on what I mentioned before, a personal recommendation."

"Okay, Roland. I'll see what I can do," Adam said, setting aside his pen. "I'll get back to you as soon as I turn up something significant."

The elderly man rose carefully from his chair, snatched his cane, and left, leaving Adam to ponder his next move. It was a small amount of info to work with...a name and a school...but plenty enough to get him started. He was confident he could track down the whereabouts of Staci Carew in short order and pass on his findings. He then could move on to his next case, satisfied he had fulfilled the favor to reconnect a World War II vet with his first love. Yep, he would quickly finish the case and be done with it, or so he thought.

CHAPTER TWO

ADAM SPENT THE GREATER PART OF HIS EARLY MORNING journey to Eastern Pasco County conjuring up images of what life along the state's rural roads must have been like circa the early 1940s. Far fewer inhabitants for one thing, he reckoned, as he observed the passing landscape through the window of his red pickup. For another, automobiles were easily distinguishable from the other, though cars on the road were fewer in number due to the "No Pleasure Driving" edicts brought about by the gasoline shortages of the war years.

As it turned out, the driving restrictions almost ended up destroying the state's tourist business. Still, some things never change, like the ostentatious roadside billboards proclaiming to passing motorists the world's largest whatever that lies ahead. And ever present, then as now, the Florida sun baking relentlessly the life and land below. Ready to bring the scene back to the present, he punched on the pickup's radio where Garth Brooks was here, there, and everywhere on the dial.

Approaching his destination, he followed the direction of a highway signpost and took an exit that fed into a scarred, two-lane asphalt road leading up to Highland Hills Prep Academy, a single gray-colored edifice planted on the crest of one of the many rolling hills characteristic of the surrounding countryside. A circular drive fed into an adjacent parking lot fronting the stone structure, shaded on all sides by tall oak trees. He parked his truck and entered the building's marble-floored foyer, feeling at once like he had stepped prematurely into middle age. For several minutes, he was the sole adult in sight as students roamed about the hallways and entrance way, chattering up a storm while paying him no heed.

At last, a rotund older woman wearing a lavender-colored blouse and beige skirt emerged from the milieu. She shuffled in his direction, her skirt swishing with her every stride. "Mr. Fraley?" she asked, a pleasant smile creasing her puffy face.

"Yes, that's me," he responded, taking her extended hand.

"I'm Loretta Flynn, the alumni representative you spoke with over the phone."

He had called in advance to check on whether there was someone to speak to regarding an alumnus of the school and on the availability of past yearbooks. In so doing, he was transferred to the "alumni lady," as the switchboard operator termed her.

"If you follow me, we can get started," she said in a cheerful tone.

Adam trailed her to a small office situated aside the entrance way. On entering he noticed two yearbooks resting on a desk "Have a seat," she said, motioning to a straight-back chair fronting her work station.

"I brought you the 1942 and 1943 editions," she said, nudging the maroon-colored tomes in his direction.

He started with the '43 volume, turning to the index in the back. He scanned a number of entries before returning his attention to the alumni lady who was observing him as if proctoring an exam. "There are no female students listed in the index," he said.

"At that time the boys' and girls' schools were separate," she explained, repeating what Westwood said. "The girls' school was called St. Scholastica. It was a companion school to Highland Hills, though at the time, it did not issue a yearbook. Many of the girls, however, appear in the boys' book, usually in the sections covering the extra-curricular activities, like cheer-leading, homecoming festivities, dances, and the like."

Adam resumed leafing through the sections suggested by Ms. Flynn. Occasionally, his attention was drawn to the boxed mini ads of local businesses, solely comprised of name, address, and three-digit phone number. "Miller Motors, 605 Commercial Street, phone 420," or "Crosby Brothers Hardware, 410 Main Street, phone 280." Simple signs of a bygone era, he mused.

It was the homecoming events section where Adam struck pay dirt, specifically the photo of the queen and her escort. "Queen Staci Carew reigns over the homecoming dance" read the caption under a shot of her sitting on her throne. Behind her stood her escort, identified as Paul Madden, captain of the football team.

By 1940s standards or 1990s, Staci was a looker, seen even in a simple black-and-white rendering. From her thick, wavy dark hair and deep-set eyes, to her svelte figure, she fit the definition of photogenic, Adam opined. No wonder Westwood was smitten with her.

"What's the name of the girl you're looking for?" the alumni lady asked, curiosity finally getting the best of her. "Maybe I can help you find her."

"Her name is Staci Carew and I've already found her," he said, tapping the page he was on.

"Staci Carew or Kati Carew?" she asked in response.

"Say again?"

"Staci Carew or Kati Carew?" she repeated, underscoring the pronunciations of the first names.

Adam recalled the spelling Westwood had given him. "Staci," he said, turning around the yearbook page and pointing to her homecoming photo.

"Yes, that's Staci."

"But there's also a Kati, you say? Were they related?"

The alumni lady leaned back in her chair and folded her arms. "They were fraternal twins. Unfortunately, Kati died in a tragic accident during her senior year."

"Is she in this yearbook?"

"No. Kati was not the social butterfly her sister was."

"The accident occurred after the yearbook's publication?"

"Yes, right after, or else I'm sure her passing would have been noted."

"She's not in an earlier yearbook?" Adam asked, patting the 1942 edition on the desk.

"Not that I recall."

"Do you know what caused the accident?"

"I don't recall the details, other than it occurred on a bridge. She was missing for a while before they discovered her body in the river."

"What river?"

"The Withlacoochee."

"Did you know the girls?"

"I was a couple of years behind them, but yes, I knew them. Like me, they were 'town girls.'"

"Meaning what?"

The alumni lady unfolded her arms and rested them on the desk. "In case you didn't know, Highland Hills Academy and St. Scholastica were primarily boarding schools, before and after they were unified. The girls who reside locally were referred to as the town girls."

Adam flipped through a few more pages of the yearbook, landing on a photo of the cheer-leading squad, their skirts reaching to the shins, their arms stretched to the sky in a mock cheer. Among them was Staci, described in the caption as the team captain.

"Whatever became of Staci?" Adam asked.

"She became a wife and mother. She was here for a class reunion several years back."

Adam harbored little personal interest in school reunions, though he once attended one for his elementary school organized by students, for the sole reason it had more to do with the neighborhood than the school. The fact was he had more of a lasting affinity for the kids next door or down the block than those from across town or out of state who showed up for the high school and college affairs.

"Where's she living now?"

"In the Tampa area, I believe. Her name is now Staci Ballard. She's married to a man by the name of Bob Ballard. That's about all I can tell you. We are not allowed to give out addresses or phone numbers."

"Understandable," he said. "Can't be too careful nowadays."

Adam, in fact, was aware of stalking cases in which it later came to light the perpetrators had checked school yearbooks during the course of their search.

"May I ask, what is your interest in Staci?"

"I'm working as a proxy for another fellow. He is a senior citizen too frail to conduct a search."

"He has a romantic or sentimental interest in Staci?"

"Had one."

"His purpose is to find her?"

"Not so much to find her as to learn what became of her," Adam replied in an effort to ease her concern.

"Did he attend Highland Hills?"

"No, he attended Chapel College, which I understand is close by."

"The next hill over," she said with a tilt of the head.

Adam thanked her for the information and told her he would pass it on to his client. As he headed for his pickup, he reflected on what he had just learned. He was reminded of how often in his search for answers, the answers invariably led to more questions, in this case a big one. Why would Roland Westwood fail to mention Staci Carew had a twin sister, a critical bit of information in a lost love search?

Back on the road, Adam stopped at a filling station to top off his tank and check for the nearest sheriff's department station. "Keep heading east on the road you're on," the attendant informed him. "It's about a twenty-minute ride further on."

Twenty minutes later, he was sitting at the desk of a man who introduced himself as Sergeant Rick Cooper, inquiring whether there were any records of a fatal bridge accident that occurred in 1943.

Cooper raised his eyebrows. "Well, that in itself must be a record for this station," he said, his sharp features matching his sharply appearing uniform. "I don't recall anyone coming into this station since it opened requesting a record going back that far. Was it a death investigation?"

"I believe so. It apparently was determined to be an accident."

"Our records are all housed in a separate building not too far from here. You can either hop over there or I can see if the record is available on the computer. From what I understand, all records have not been converted to digital format."

"Would you mind checking? I'm looking to save time," Adam said, sensing the sergeant's willingness to assist.

"No, not at all, but first I'll need some information, starting with your name, address, and phone number."

Adam provided the info, throwing in his occupation to keep everything above board.

"You say this occurred in 1943?" he asked, pencil and paper in hand.

"Yes, but I don't have the exact date."

"Fatal accident on a bridge. Do you know what bridge?"

"No, but the river was the Withlacoochee."

"Do you know the name of the person killed?"

"That I do know. Her name is Kati Carew. Kati is spelled K-A-T-I. She was a student at St. Scholastica School."

"Good. That should help. Anything else?"

"Sorry, that's the extent of it. She did have a twin sister named Staci, spelled S-T-A-C-I."

For several minutes, Adam set back and watched as the sergeant alternately started and stopped his striking of keys, occasionally pausing to study the material he retrieved.

"Found it," he abruptly said following one lengthy pause. "Not much to the report, it looks like," he continued, motioning to the screen before ticking off the pertinent points. "It states here the office received a report of a missing girl and immediately assigned an investigative team led by Detective Glen Martin to the case. The team subsequently found the body of Kati Carew floating face down in the

Withlacoochee River a short distance downstream from an abandoned bridge. She was wearing a leotard. Deputies found a pair of shoes and bike shorts belonging to Miss Carew next to one of the bridge railings. The span is a favorite spot for teenagers to go bridge jumping due to the relatively deep channel at that particular point. According to friends and family, Miss Carew often engaged in the activity, though there were no witnesses placing her at the scene on the day of the incident. The victim had been missing for approximately twenty-four hours when her parents notified the department of her disappearance. The coroner's report noted a deep bruise on the victim's inner left thigh as well as a second severe bruise on the side of her head. The coroner stated the wounds likely occurred when the victim accidentally fell and hit the support beams. The blow to the head in all probability knocked her unconscious. The cause of death was listed as an accidental drowning. There was no evidence of foul play."

Cooper shoved his chair back from the desk. "Want a copy?"

Adam nodded. "Strange she was out bridge jumping alone, don't you think?" he casually asked. "With teenagers it's usually a group outing."

The deputy shrugged. "You may have a point there," he said, ripping off a copy of the report from the printer and handing it to him. "If you don't mind me asking, what is your interest in this case?"

"I have a client who wants to know whatever became of Miss Carew," Adam answered, fudging the truth.

"You might be interested in knowing the detective mentioned in the report, Glen Martin, is still living in the area."

"Retired, I presume."

"Yes, but he spends a good deal of his time here at the station reminiscing about olden days on the force. I'm sure he would be glad to answer any questions you might have about the case. You want me to give him a call?"

"Sure," Adam replied, jumping at the offer.

Cooper snatched the phone, punched in a number, and tapped his pencil on the desk with scissored fingers. "Glen? Rick Cooper here at the station. I'm fine. Say, Glen, there's an out-of-town private detective here looking for information on a case you worked on back in 1943. He's sitting right across the desk from me right now. Which one? It was an investigation into the death of a young girl by the name of Kati Carew. She apparently fell from a bridge and ended up drowning. You do remember? Would you be willing to meet with this fellow to discuss the case? You would…Seven o'clock tomorrow morning in this office."

Cooper peeked at Adam over the receiver, flashing him a grin that said Martin was setting the time and place for the meeting. Adam nodded his agreement.

"Thanks Glen," Cooper said and hung up the phone. "He'll see you in the morning," the deputy said to his visitor, closing the session.

———

Back on the road, Adam first stopped at a burger joint for a late lunch before seeking out the nearest motel, finding one less than a mile from the sheriff's station. A change of plans was in order; one of the reasons he always carried a change of clothing in his pickup. Once settled into his room, he called Tamra. "I have a big favor to ask of you," he said.

"We've got to slow down these exchanges of favors," she replied in jest.

"Noelle has a softball game after school today. Could you accompany her to the game? She's expecting me to pick her up after class."

"I'm sure she'd rather have her daddy accompany her, but yes, I'll be glad to do it. What's up?"

"What's come up is a couple of leads I need to follow through on. Plus, I have an interview scheduled here early in the morning. They require an overnight stay. I should be back in the office by mid-afternoon. Oh, and I have an assignment for you," he added. "I'd like for you to find any information you can on a woman by the name of

Staci Ballard. That's S-T-A-C-I. She's married and living in the Tampa area. She's in her early seventies or so. Her maiden name is Staci Carew. She's originally from the Eastern Pasco County region."

"Got it."

"Again, thanks much for playing chaperon and tell Noelle I'll make it up to her."

"No problem. We'll have fun."

———

Adam took a shower, donned his spare set of clothes, and retired to the motel lobby where he sunk himself deep into the comfort of a lounge chair. He proceeded to pour over the sheriff's report for items not mentioned in Cooper's quick screen scan. Mostly cursory stuff, he concluded. What did catch his interest was an appended roster of persons who were interviewed in the course of the investigation. Among them were Roland Westwood and Staci Carew, identified respectively as college student and sister of the victim. Several other students, as well as Kati's parents, were also listed. Two entries were of particular interest to Adam—Marcia Friedman, School Guidance Counselor and Anna Korlov, owner of World Gymnastics, Inc. They were names of individuals he would bring up with Martin for possible follow-up.

Adam set aside the report. A sliver of guilt had penetrated his concentration. Missing his daughter's softball game was unbecoming to a parent, a single one at that. Going the adoption route was not a choice universally cheered by family and friends alike. Yet, of all the decisions in his life, none could approach it in generating a pure joy and deep sense of purpose in life in him. Still, here he sat, frozen in place by an obvious omission in a client's story that could be nothing more than a simple oversight. The fact was, his core assignment was nearly complete. He had found Staci Carew and in short order Tamra would have an address and phone number to go with the name. Case closed and into the ephemeral file it would go. Wasn't that his belief all along? Restless, he snatched the report and resumed his review.

CHAPTER THREE

SERGEANT COOPER ESCORTED THE TWO DETECTIVES TO A cubbyhole of a conference room, furnished with a government-issued metal table and folding chairs, only two of which were needed, Cooper having excused himself from the session due to a prior commitment.

"I appreciate you taking the time to discuss this case with me, Detective Martin," Adam said, tapping the sheriff's report he had dropped on the table before taking a seat.

"My pleasure," the crusty-faced veteran said in a coarse voice, "though I'm surprised this is the one up for discussion after all these years. I don't have it ranked high on my most memorable list."

Martin's loose-fitting look in clothing conformed to the popular image of the Florida retiree. An over-sized blue flannel shirt, its sleeves furled to the forearms, bulky khaki shorts, and wide, scuffed boots concealed a medium frame. The concealing extended to his scalp where remnants of russet hair were carefully arranged in comb-over style.

Adam's intention coming into the session was to avoid playing the role of Monday-morning quarterback. As the lead detective in the investigation, Martin was unlikely to take kindly to an out-of-town private eye playing critic to his work. No, Adam was simply there to gather information.

"What in the world stirred your interest in this case?" Martin asked right off.

"A client of mine once had a brief relationship with Staci Carew. He had always wondered what became of her, so after fifty years or so of wondering, he hired me to find out."

"Why the interest in the circumstances of her sister's death?"

"It's part of the story. I'm sure my client would be interested in the incident. After all, fraternal twins are inseparable. So should their stories be."

"What's your client's name, if you don't mind me asking?"

"Funny you should ask, his name appears in the report," Adam replied, nodding to the document. "Roland Westwood is his name."

Martin picked up the report and casually scanned the appendix for the name. "Oh, yeah, Staci's boyfriend," he said upon finding it. "Nice kid. You say he would be interested in learning of the incident. Shouldn't he have already been aware of it?"

"Probably so," Adam replied, at once covering his misstep. "I could well be duplicating what he already knows, but it's my style to make my client aware of everything I turn up."

The 'nice kid' reference Adam found interesting, considering Martin could not have been much older than Westwood at the time. Was the young, inexperienced detective assigned to lead the case young and inexperienced enough to take things at face value? Perhaps the department had no other choice in picking Martin due to the wartime manpower shortage, he speculated.

"In reading the report, the detective in me was surprised there were no witnesses to the event. Kids normally don't go bridge jumping alone, do they?"

"That was one of the first questions we asked," Martin said. "The answer from people in the know was that it was not at all unusual for Kati. She frequently went alone."

"You say 'people in the know.' They were her friends, classmates, parents?"

"As a matter of fact, it came from two of the people who knew her best—her sister Staci and Roland Westwood, your client. They both were adamant in saying it was not out of the ordinary."

"As a rule, they didn't accompany her on the jumps?"

"Correct. It was a moot point anyway," Martin said. "If I recall right, Staci and her boyfriend had gone on a trail hike over near Dade City that morning."

"How did Kati get to the bridge?"

"She borrowed her parents' car. It was found parked near the bridge."

"Did she tell them where she was going?"

"Yes, to the bridge."

"But no specifics as to what for or whether she was going by herself."

"No, though they assumed it was for some bridge jumping."

"The report says her shoes and shorts were found on the bridge. What was she wearing when she was found in the river?" Adam asked, trying mightily not to sound like an interrogator.

"She was wearing a leotard, which in those days doubled as a swimsuit. She was found floating face down in a carpet of water hyacinths. Dragonflies were buzzing about her."

Okay, so he threw in that last bit of info for dramatic effect, something Adam could have done without. "Suicide was ruled out?" he asked.

"Yep. According to everyone—friends, family, teachers—she had no reason to be despondent, nor did she give any inkling she was. On the contrary, she had a new boyfriend." Martin paused to check the report. "Yeah, his name was Paul Madden. He was another reason she was in a positive frame of mind."

"Where was he at the time of the incident?"

"He was out of town, down in the Keys on a quick trip with his family."

The image of the homecoming queen Staci Carew and her escort Paul Madden in the school yearbook flashed into Adam's mind. He was tempted to ask Martin if he was aware of the prior relationship between Staci and Madden but decided not to, figuring that was now a moot point also, given the content of the original report. It was apparent to Adam that Westwood had not told him of the relationship for the simple reason he did not want to give Martin any reason to dig further into the incident.

"Marcia Friedman is listed as school counselor," Adam said, nodding to the report. "What did she have to say about Kati?"

"Nothing but positive stuff. Great girl, great student, great everything, including a great outlook on life. When we brought up the possibility of suicide, she, like everyone else, threw cold water on the notion."

"Anna Korlov...she's listed as the gymnastics coach. Where does she fit in?"

"Kati was a student at her gym. Korlov was the owner, operator, and served as Kati's instructor. From what we were told, she was Korlov's prized pupil, an accomplished gymnast who had a bright future in the sport. It was one more reason for her to be in a positive frame of mind."

By all means. Speak well of the dead, particularly the young in the aftermath of tragedy, Adam ruminated. "Yeah, put any negativity that might be associated with the event to rest along with the deceased. Let it eventually float to the surface, if it must, like a lifeless body from the deep once the cries from the dead can no longer be ignored." Words he vividly recalled from a reading of the literature on the subject of cold cases.

"Is Anna Korlov still around?" he asked.

"Not sure if she's still around but her business is."

"Do you know its location?"

"Sure do. I drive by it nearly every day. It's on the main highway about five miles north of Zepherhills. It's hard to miss. You'll see what looks like an old airport hangar with 'World Gymnastics' in large block lettering on its side."

"And the location of the bridge?"

"Take this road we're on ten miles further east where you'll run into a county road intersection. Follow the county road south about a mile and right before you cross the river you'll intersect with an unmarked power line road. Take a left onto the power line road and a mile later you'll be able to see the remains of the bridge through the trees and brush on your right. Officially, it's still an abandoned bridge."

"Why don't they tear it down?"

"Not sure, though nowadays it seems nearly everything still standing from the pre-second world war era is argued to be historical. I guess that also makes an old geezer like me historical," he added with a trace of levity.

"What's the name of the river?"

"The Withlacoochee," Martin said, affecting a southern drawl. "It means crooked river. The thing runs from the south to the north, from its origin over in the Green Swamp in Hernando County to the Gulf. There are long stretches of remote wilderness along its path. There's also a Withlacoochee River up in North Florida. People are frequently confusing the two."

"Like twins," Adam quipped.

"Like twins," the retired detective repeated. "By the way, the Withlacoochee is known for its small bass, in case you're interested in engaging in a second fishing expedition," he said with a wry smile.

"One last question," Adam said, ignoring the jab. "Is there a public library close by?"

"Very close by," Martin responded. "In fact, you can walk to it from here. It's right around the corner. There are several county government operations in this complex. The library is one of them. They closed down the old one and relocated here."

———

Adam found the library, which appeared to be housed in a converted office building of some kind. He asked the librarian if there was a local newspaper and how far it went back in time. "There is only one...a weekly newspaper called the Inland Courier," she said. "I believe it goes back to the 1930s. We do have the back holdings on microfilm," she added. "How far did you want to go back?"

"I'd like to see the 1943 issues," he said.

The librarian retrieved a roll of microfilm and set it up on a reader for him. "Since it's a weekly, you shouldn't have much trouble scrolling through a year's worth," she said, leaving him to his business.

Adam scrolled through the first two months of the year with no results. The third month yielded his first hit, an article not on the sports page but a feature in the local section. A striking black and white photo of Kati accompanied the article. A fraternal twin, she bore without a doubt, a definite resemblance to her sister, though beautiful in her own way. For whatever reason, Adam found the photo surprisingly emotive. There was an aura about her not even the black and white rendering could diminish. The photographer, to his credit, chose not to settle for a posed shot. Instead, he captured her in a candid moment of reflection as she stood aside the balance beam, mentally preparing for an exercise routine according to the caption. She had a hand gently resting on the beam, as if it was a friend, not an enemy. Written on her face was a depth of feeling well beyond her years. She was someone you would like to get to know, someone whose beauty was no barrier to her soul. Such was the representation that even the most casual observer could not help but wonder what thoughts dwelt in the quiet of that heart of hers. Perhaps it was the private detective in him, the need he felt to empathize with her that drew him into the photo. Or was it something outside the frame–something he was not seeing, the untold part of her story–that commanded his attention?

Small town girl chases big dream.

Kati Carew is not your typical teenage girl when it comes to interests outside her normal school activities. She readily admits boys and clothes do not rank at the top of her leisure pursuits. On the contrary, becoming a world champion in women's gymnastics is much more on the talented San Antonio girl's mind these days.

Kati's dream had its origin in a visit she made several years ago to her favorite local hangout, the public library. "I was looking for books on basic exercise programs, but they were all out," she said, "so I picked up this little book on women's gymnastics, thinking it might offer some basic fitness tips."

Not only did the book provide Kati recommended exercises, it introduced her to the sport of gymnastics. "I sat down and read the entire book in the library," she said. The opening chapter on the history of the sport in particular captured her attention. "I was amazed at the growth in the popularity of the sport, especially overseas, and the opportunity it provided young girls to perform on the international stage."

According to Kati, the author of the book underscored the corresponding lack of interest in the sport in the United States, a condition the author felt could only be remedied by the development of a winning presence on the international stage.

"The author also pointed out that women's gymnastics was likely to become an Olympic sport," Kati said, "so I decided the best way to help spread the popularity of the sport here was to aim for an Olympic medal. I talked it over with my parents and they were very encouraging. They decided to enroll me in a training program at World Gymnastics gym."

Kati's coach at World Gymnastics is Anna Korlov, the owner of the facility. "She has made great progress," Korlov said. "She definitely has world class potential and most of all the determination and focus to achieve her goal. I may be biased in saying this, but I believe she has the talent to capture a gold medal."

Kati already has made waves in the sport, placing first in several regional contests. Her specialty is the balance beam, one of the more difficult gymnastic events. Based on her recent performances, she is expected to qualify for the nationals.

"She's come a long way from playing on monkey bars and rings," her coach said. "She still has a long road to travel, but the future for her looks bright."

Adam scrolled through several more months of the Inland Courier until he landed on an article covering the bridge incident. It was accompanied by the same photo of Kati Carew that appeared in the earlier feature on her. A photo of a boyish looking Glen Martin, identified in the caption as a detective working the case, was also included. The story itself, Adam learned in reading, was mostly a rehash of the original sheriff's report. A search through the remainder of the paper turned up nothing, at which point he rewound the reel and returned it to the librarian. Before he left, however, he needed to satisfy a curiosity. He checked the shelves for volumes on gymnastics. It turned out there were three. Two were recent publications. The third was a much older work, its cover worn, and pages faded. He slipped the small tome from its resting place, found a table, and began to browse it. He noted the copyright date to be 1943. Why the library had yet to weed the volume from its holdings, he could only speculate. From the general condition of the collection, there appeared to be very little weeding at all, perhaps due to tight collection development budgets over the years.

When the library was moved to its present location, they obviously took everything with them, he concluded, including the vintage volumes. In browsing the book, Adam discovered that the first chapter was devoted entirely to the history of the sport. He knew then and there he was looking at the same book that gave birth to Kati's dream. He absentmindedly skimmed the remainder of the pages, believing what he held in his hand was not so much basic text on a sport as it was a relic from a young girl's past.

———

The lobby of World Gymnastics, Inc. was a hive of energized youth. Groups of mostly young girls, accompanied by their guardians, were entering and exiting in an excitable state, buoyed in spirit by a sport growing ever more popular with middle and upper-class families alike.

Adam eased his way through the foot traffic to a service counter where a middle-aged, pixie-cut blond in red Capri pants and flowing white top greeted him. "Can I help you, sir?"

"Yes, I'd like to speak to Anna Korlov," he said directly, aware he may be asking to speak to the dead.

"Do you mean Linda Korlov?" the woman asked back. "Anna

Korlov no longer works here. Linda is her daughter and currently is in charge of the business."

Adam was about to curse his luck when a woman waiting next to him at the service counter voluntarily jumped in. "I just saw Anna step into Linda's office a minute ago," she said.

"She does drop in on occasion," the clerk said, picking up a counter phone to check if that was the case. "Linda, does your mother happen to be back there? She is. There's a gentleman here who would like to speak to her. Just a minute." The clerk wedged the receiver between her shoulder and chin, turning her attention back to Adam. "May I tell her who you are and what this is about?" she asked.

"My name is Adam Fraley. I'm a private detective. I'd like to speak to her about a girl named Kati Carew," he said.

The clerk repeated the request over the phone. "Yes, okay, will do," she said and hung up the phone. "Mrs. Korlov will meet you in the spectator section," she said and gave him directions.

Adam entered the main floor of the cavernous gym through a side door. Immediately, he was exposed to an array of apparatus, including trampolines, parallel bars, horizontal bars, uneven bars, balance beams, rings, and pommel horses, all arranged in functional order. Randomly spaced throughout the workout area, like throw rugs, were orange and blue mats.

He circled the perimeter of the room until he reached the spectators section, a recessed area of rising metal benches equivalent to a single section of grandstand. He took a seat on the bottom bench to await Anna Korlov, at the same time observing the young gymnasts go through their routines under the watchful eyes of their coaches.

Shortly, she appeared, a woman of small stature with cat-like opal eyes, pale skin, thin-boned cheeks, and narrow neck. Her dyed-black hair was pulled tightly into a bun. She was dressed in black slacks and white blouse.

"Mrs. Korlov," Adam said, rising to greet her.

"Mr. Fraley, I understand you wish to see me," she said in a pronounced Eastern European accent before helping herself to a seat on the bench.

"Yes, I appreciate your seeing me," he said, joining her on the bench. "I know I'm going far back in time, but I've been told you might provide me background information on a former student of yours by the name of Kati Carew."

"I was told you are a private investigator. Can you tell me what this is about?"

Adam appended his stock answer to the question, stating he was on assignment for a client, who was a childhood friend of her sister, Staci Carew, and how in the course of his investigation the subject of her sister came up.

Her eyes brightened at the explanation. "Oh, my. You bring up a favorite subject of mine," she said. "I never tire of telling the story of Kati Carew. Do you wish to hear it?"

"Please," Adam said.

"First, let me talk about myself a bit," she said with a chuckle. "My husband and I immigrated to the United States in 1939 from Czechoslovakia after the NAZI's incorporated part of the country into Germany. I was a gymnastics coach in my native country and very much wanted to pursue the profession over here. Gymnastics was not nearly as popular in the States as it was in Eastern Europe. However, I looked at it as an opportunity to raise the level of competition in much the same way as basketball coaches here accept job offers to take over coaching duties for overseas national teams.

"I opened a small gym up the road from here with earnings I had accumulated and saved in the old country. I had no idea whether I could make a go of it, but as it turned out, there were enough parents interested in enrolling their children in our program to initially keep the business afloat.

"One of the parents was Kati's mother who enrolled her and her twin sister into the program. Both girls were cheerleaders at their school and were interested in perfecting their tumbling skills.

"It was apparent from the outset one sister was more interested than the other in becoming a full-fledged gymnast and that was Kati.

Staci, her sister, was more of a social butterfly and obviously was not interested in advancing beyond the basic tumbling routines. She was a cheerleader at heart and soon dropped out of the program. Kati, on the other hand, was totally committed to the program, which thrilled me to no end. The first day I saw her on the floor performing tumbling routines, I knew she had great potential. Her body control, body awareness, flexibility, and sense of timing were extraordinary for a thirteen-year-old. Moreover, and don't let people tell you it doesn't count, she was gorgeous in her appearance with her long slender lines and graceful movements. However, her most impressive quality was her determination to learn all aspects of gymnastics, beginning with its history. She spent endless hours reading up on the sport. The historical aspect ended up becoming a main motivating factor for her. Her goal was to spearhead a greater American interest in the sport."

"How did she plan on doing that?" Adam asked.

"I told her the only way to accomplish that kind of challenging goal was to capture the international spotlight by winning an Olympic gold medal. Unfortunately, women's gymnastics at the time was not an Olympic event, though a movement to add it was gaining momentum. The war years slowed the momentum, but Kati and I proceeded on the notion that once the war ended the Olympics would be back in the spotlight with women's gymnastics a big part of it."

"Kati was thirteen at the time. Isn't that considered a late age to take up the sport?" Adam asked.

"Presently, it is but not back then. Women in their twenties were winning tournaments having taken up the sport in their teens."

"So, you drew up a plan for Kati?"

"We constructed one together, one that would best suit her goal. For an American gymnast to break the monopoly the East European and Soviet Union athletes had on the sport required a level of performance that could not be ignored by foreign judges who were programmed to downplay American efforts. We decided the best way to do it was to concentrate on a single event and become so proficient at it the judges could no longer ignore the quality without looking foolish."

"I understand her specialty was the balance beam."

"Yes, the balance beam, the most demanding of events. It requires an advanced skill many gymnasts to this day fail to achieve."

"Did Kati have the fundamentals down to perform at that level?"

"Yes. Her cheer-leading experience, though rudimentary, gave her a head start. When she arrived at my school, she already had honed her tumbling skills, handstands, hand walks, and cartwheels. She performed them with great ease. More than anything, it was her willingness to learn that catapulted her to greater heights. I gave her many of my training films and training manuals I had brought over from the old country. She spent hours on end studying them."

"She became proficient at the balance beam. Was there anything in particular that you felt would capture the attention of the judges?"

"Yes, the most difficult maneuver, the back handspring. It causes more anxiety among gymnasts than just about any other move. Back tumbling on a floor mat is one thing. Back tumbling on a four-inch wide beam is an entirely different matter, as you can imagine. You see that girl on the balance beam over there?" she asked, pointing to the far side of the floor. "She's practicing spins, front flips, switch leaps, and split leaps. Mastering those basic moves is a requirement to move on to the advanced level."

"How do you master the back handspring?" Adam asked, bewildered how anyone could perform such a move in a highly competitive environment. He was an Olympic junkie himself and recalled the hours he spent in front of the television, marveling at the women gymnasts competing in the event.

"You start on a line on the floor. Next you practice the maneuver on a floor beam or low beam. You then move to a medium beam and finally to the high beam."

"Are their methods to overcoming the fear factor?"

"You see those mats scattered about the floor?" she asked with a sweep of her hand. "They are piled alongside the beam as a safety net until the gymnast gains enough confidence to perform without them.

It doesn't take much to lose your balance. The gymnast's objective is to minimize the chances of making a mistake. For instance, the hands should be placed one in front of the other on the beam when performing a handspring. Trying to place them side by side on a four-inch width surface is likely to cause the gymnast to slip from the beam."

"How long did it take Kati to perfect the back handspring?"

"A year, and not only did she perfect it, she blew away the degree of difficulty by adding to her routine a third backflip without the aid of the beam."

"You mean with no hands?"

"Yes…something that was not accomplished at the Olympic level until the Russian girl Olga Korbut did it in 1972. If you recall, her performance electrified the gymnastics world."

"Kati was way ahead of her time, wasn't she?" Adam said, his eyes following a gymnast working the beam.

"Oh, yes she was. I will never forget the day she first performed it without the aid of mats and me standing by ready to catch her in case of a fall."

"This was in a competition?"

"No, it was during a practice session at my first gym, a tiny facility up the road a mile or so. There were several students on hand to witness it. All of them took a break to watch Kati, aware she was going to attempt it for the first time as part of her routine. I can see her now standing on the beam, preparing to execute it, confident as always." Anna slapped her hands together. "Bang…one backflip followed by a second backflip, and a third without the use of hands, all executed in one flawless, fluid, rhythmic motion. The other students jumped for joy. They knew the difficulty of it. Kati was not only an athlete, she was an artist as well. I knew at that moment our goal for her was no longer a pipe dream. Look out world, here she comes!"

"What was next for her?"

"We entered her in a select number of regional competitions and she shined in all of them. By the time she turned seventeen, the national gymnastics community was starting to take notice."

"The pressure of competition did not get to her?"

"No," she said emphatically. "The Ernest Hemingway phrase 'grace under pressure' comes to mind when describing her performances. It is the critical ingredient in every successful athlete's career. No matter how well they perform in practice, they have to repeat it in front of the judges."

"Did she do the back handspring in competition?"

"Yes, but not the no-hands one. We were saving it for an important regional competition that was coming up. We wanted to spring it as a surprise. Unfortunately, it was never to be." Anna paused in her story, her memories overwhelming her composure. "She was such a natural."

"Did Kati have any boyfriends?" Adam asked, steering the conversation sharply in another direction.

"I don't know. I suppose she was like most teenage girls in that regard, though her social life must have been limited what with all the time she put into gymnastics."

"Do you recall a boy by the name of Roland Westwood?"

Korlov furrowed her brow in thought. "No, I can't say I do. Was he a friend of Kati?"

"Not sure," Adam replied. "How did she and her sister get along?"

"Fine, as far as I could tell. Like I said, her sister dropped out of the program before reaching an advanced level. She seemed more interested in the social aspects of cheer leading as opposed to the individual lifestyle required of the gymnast."

"Did law enforcement officials interview you regarding the circumstances surrounding Kati's death?"

"Yes, but there was little I could tell them other than she was in an excellent frame of mind and was looking forward to pursuing her career in gymnastics."

"One last question if I may," Adam said. "As talented as Kati was on the beam, did it not strike you as odd that she somehow lost her balance on the bridge which resulted in her fall? She was, after all, a master at keeping it."

Anna gave a slight shrug of the shoulders. "To be honest, I was so shaken by the news of her death, I didn't pay much attention to the details of how it occurred. All I heard was that she accidentally fell from the bridge. But you may have a point there. It would be unusual for her to lose her balance, barring an unexpected circumstance."

"Hey, Mrs. Korlov," a young gymnast leaving the floor called to her. The veteran coach waved and smiled her greeting back.

For a brief time, Adam and Anna sat quietly, absorbing the energy coming from the floor as practice routines were carried out amid the chatter of coaches and their charges echoing through the building.

His questioning completed, Adam excused himself, thanking the matriarch of World Gymnastics for her time and input. "I'll leave you my card in case any additional information comes to mind," he said. Whereupon, he departed, leaving her alone with her thoughts. From the winsome cast to her face, they appeared to be lingering on the small gym up the road and her once prized pupil.

———

Adam glanced down at the directions to the Withlacoochee bridge Martin had scribbled down for him. He followed the roads, new and old, past rows of citrus groves, shallow swamps filled with cattails and arrowheads, pockets of pine thickets, and a succession of small lakes until he reached the final stretch of the power line road and a line of cypress trees through which he spotted the river and abandoned bridge. He pulled to a stop aside the road and hopped from his truck into a brilliant sunshine, blinding him for a moment. Trudging through some heavy brush, he stepped around a couple of weed-strewn mounds and strolled between two stands of cypress trees to the bridge approach, scattering a flock of grazing white ibis to the wind along the way. Pausing to gather his bearings, he stepped to the side of the span to assess the structure. It was a concrete bridge, extending maybe a hundred feet in length, supported by two horizontal girders approximately thirty-five feet high. Concrete barriers were attached to the deck slab. Running atop the barriers were three-tiered metal railings. Strung across the bridge approach was a two-beam wooden barrier with a No Trespassing sign attached to it. Adam slipped between the beams and onto the bridge, at which point he began a slow walk across it.

Though still in one piece, the bridge understandably displayed numerous signs of deterioration. The concrete barriers and road bed were cracked and corroded from end to end. With few exceptions sections of the metal railings were either bent, stained, or rusted. Halfway across Adam stopped to look over the railing at the languid, dark brown river below. He figured it to be a forty-foot drop. The stream appeared to narrow at this point in its flow, creating a greater depth, thereby making it an ideal spot for bridge jumping. Planted alongside the shoreline was a bleached-out canoe trail sign. Further upstream, a quarter mile or so, stood a train trestle. He decided to give it a closer look.

Tramping through more thick brush, he was thankful he had donned his jeans and boots for the trek. "No telling what you can kick up in this stuff," he mumbled to himself. No sooner had he thought it than a good ol' Florida rat snake slithered across his path before disappearing into the weeds. Finally, passing a large wooden log reaching into the stream upon which two turtles were sunning themselves and circling around another "No Trespassing" sign, he reached the trestle approach. Given the good condition of the trestle, track, and cross ties, he concluded the road was still in operation. Standing in the middle of the trestle, he had a clear view of the abandoned bridge. What were the odds, he wondered, of a train passing the very day and time a young girl was bridge jumping a quarter mile away? He envisioned a steam engine trailing a chain of cars across the trestle but, alas, snorting enough black smoke to snuff out a clear view of the span running parallel to it. Throw in the likelihood of an inattentive crew and the odds became longer.

Having talked himself out of a train crew sighting, he headed back to the abandoned bridge for one last look. Traversing the opposite bank from the one he'd hiked up on, he encountered even thicker vegetation, at one point halting to delicately pick a basket full of cockle burrs from his jeans. Soldiering on, beads of perspiration began to form on his forehead, as twigs crunched and snapped under his feet and limbs of trees slapped him in the face. Plowing through one particularly difficult thicket, he happened upon a large clearing. "Whoa!" he whooped, stopping in his tracks, for standing directly in front of him were a man and a woman wearing nothing but wide smiles on their faces.

"Sorry, I didn't mean to interrupt," Adam said lamely while attempting to avert his eyes.

"No need to be sorry," the man said. "You're welcome to join us."

The only joining he could ponder at the moment was that of cockle burrs with an abundance of naked flesh.

"We're the Lacoochee Nature Club, the oldest all-natural nature club in the state," the woman volunteered, as if making a membership pitch. "We date back to the turn of the century. Every Friday morning, you'll find us right here. You sure you don't want to hang with us a while?"

From the corner of his eye, Adam caught other members of the group milling about the clearing. "I'm afraid I'm not dressed for the occasion," he quipped.

The woman at once flashed him a big smile. "That's easily remedied," she responded.

"Sorry, maybe another day. Right now, I must be on my way," he said, stepping away to resume his hike. "I'm in the middle of a survey."

Back on the bridge, he couldn't help but notice several members of the nature club had slipped from the clearing to frolic in the river. Wary of being mistaken for a voyeur, he returned to the business at hand, leaning over a section of railing to check the support structure below. In doing so, his attention was grabbed by the railing itself, specifically its flat top. Though generally rusted and discolored, it featured a brushed finish on its surface, probably achieved by means of a sanding machine, the original purpose of which no doubt was to apply a textured grip to the stainless steel.

Adam took a step back to envision the stretch of railing as it might have appeared a half century ago. Hurriedly, he searched his pockets for any kind of measuring tool. Scrambling for something that wasn't there, he recalled the time Tamra, in a frivolous moment, asked to see the palm of his hand to measure its exact width. When asked what the hell for, she explained she had read an article on palm reading and was interested to see if the width of his palm corresponded to the interpretation in the article and whether it jived with what she knew of him. The accuracy of the interpretation he didn't recall but the width of his palm he did. He reached out and rested it flat on the width of the railing. A perfect match…four inches.

CHAPTER FOUR

"SHE WAS WHAT?" ADAM ASKED.

"Kicked out of her softball game," Tamra replied calmly from behind her desk across the room.

"Noelle? For what?"

"Arguing balls and strikes with the plate umpire. And she was in the right. I was there to witness it."

"Right about the calls?" Adam asked.

"She was right in arguing. The umpire was calling a pitch a ball or strike before it was halfway to the plate."

"Oh, not this again," Adam snapped in frustration. "Wasn't it our landlord's father...the little league umpire, who was always pulling the same stunt before he croaked?"

"The difference is this is fast-pitch softball, not slow-pitch, and it involves your daughter."

"Maybe he was also tired of waiting for the ball to reach home plate," Adam cracked.

"As I said, Adam, this is fast-pitch we're talking about. Let me show you," she said, reaching into her desk drawer and pulling out a camcorder.

Adam rose from his desk and strolled across the room. "You have evidence?"

"Isn't that what you're always asking our clients?" she said. "Take a look at this."

Tamra held the camera to Adam's eye and hit the play button. "I was sitting behind home plate when all this was occurring. See Noelle at the plate?"

"I see her."

"Now watch the first pitch. The umpire clearly raises his right hand to indicate a strike before the pitch is even halfway to the plate. In fact, it didn't even reach the plate."

"You're right," Adam said, his eyes glued to the recorder.

Tamra lowered the camcorder. "The pitcher was throwing a lot of drop balls which are intended to look like they're coming straight across the plate but drop suddenly before reaching it. They were fooling the umpire more than they were Noelle." Tamra raised the recorder again to Adam's eye. "Now watch Noelle calmly turn and question one of the calls...bam!...that's all it took for him to eject her."

"They've got a league championship series coming up. I hope this is only a one-game suspension. How did she take it?"

Tamra placed the camcorder back into the desk. "She was disheartened. However, I told her she was in the right. I hope you don't mind, Adam, but I took the liberty of setting up a meeting with the league's supervisor of officials concerning this. I looked up the baseball rules for umpires and it clearly states, 'Wait until the play is completed before making any arm motion.' This needs to be brought to the league's attention, Adam. They talk about a code of conduct for fans. Well, they need to worry about the conduct of their own representatives."

It came as no surprise that Tamra would take up arms for his daughter. Since that day four years ago when he announced to her he was adopting Noelle, she took a keen interest in her development, on and off the field. Admittedly, his path to becoming a single parent was an uncommon one. With marriage prospects at low ebb, he began to entertain the idea of adopting a daughter. In the end it took a murder-suicide case to make it happen.

It started out as a quick trip to Colorado over the Christmas holidays to visit an old Air Force buddy. Mother nature, however, intervened in the form of a blinding snowstorm, steering him to an isolated cabin in the woods to seek directions. There to greet him was the dwelling's lone inhabitant, Noelle, who was unaware her mother had been murdered in a fit of rage by her father.

Soon after, the father took his own life, leaving Noelle an orphan. Captured by her charm, Adam instinctively knew she was the one to fill the growing void in his life.

When the case came to a close, he made the decision to pursue his dream of a daughter. With the support of friends and family, not to mention the consent of Noelle, he took the necessary legal steps to place him on the road to parenthood.

The change in lifestyle turned out not to be all that dramatic for him, with the singular exception of having to stretch his income to cover the cost of child rearing. In fact, he learned early on everything in his life was to become an investment in his daughter's health and happiness. As for his social life, it wasn't affected much, since he barely had one to begin with.

Lately, however, ever since his daughter unilaterally decided to take over management of his social life for the simple reason she wanted a mother, matters had become more complex. Up until then, balancing work with parental duties proved to be a minor issue, thanks to her self-discipline and penchant to please. A child who wanted to please a parent was a blessing he'd come to realize. Moreover, the trauma of her mother's murder, though not entirely erased, had faded into the background, replaced in large part by the fonder memories of her childhood. There was no need for a child psychologist to be consulted during the early days, as he'd once feared.

Looking back, it was an unexpected gift he'd been blessed with that Colorado Christmas and, yes, no greater gift could he have received.

Over time, Tamra became, in effect, Noelle's surrogate mother, much to his daughter's liking. He considered the bond between them no less firm than the one between him and his daughter. When he mentioned this to his former boss and designated lifetime mentor, Pete Peterson, the question was posed to Adam. "Isn't it about time you completed the bonding between you two and start a family?"

"Do I not have a family at the moment?" he'd ruminated on hearing his boss's words. He appeared to be working at it, admittedly taking a reverse approach to building one with his adoption of Noelle, not that the traditional approach was uppermost in his mind at the time of the adoption or that he was even planning a family. He sure as hell was not trying to meet a definition.

What constitutes a family, anyway, and what are dictionary definitions other than opinions of the learned? The dictionaries can't seem to keep up with the times as is. The operating phrase apparently is 'a group living under the same roof,' whether it be a man and wife, a man and wife with children, a single parent, 'descendants of a common ancestor,' and so on. In other words, a household comprised of blood relatives. If that's the case, by his estimation he fit in there somewhere, though his personal definition was more precise. The family, if he was to build one, would need a mother and not a surrogate one.

"You know what they say about office romances, Pete," he'd replied to his ex-boss's suggestion. "They're guaranteed to fracture employee relations, especially when they involve a supervisor-subordinate type situation."

"Did it ever cross your mind you might be fracturing employee relations if you don't make a move? At least shoot for a lunch or dinner date. See what happens. That is, if she doesn't die first from your asking."

"I'll take your advice under consideration," Adam had responded, cutting short the conversation.

"When is the meeting with the softball official scheduled?" he asked Tamra.

"One o'clock next Tuesday afternoon. At the league office."

"Did you dig up anything on Staci Carew?" he asked.

"Sure did," she said, tearing off a slip of paper from her desk notepad and handing it to him. "Here are the basics–home address and phone number, business address and phone number, along with the same for her husband. In case you're interested, at one time or another, she also served on the boards of directors for the local Girl Scouts, the public library system, the arts council, the mental health professionals association, the YWCA. Do you want me to go on?"

"No, I think the theme is clear. She's bordering on civil sainthood."

"Appears so. And now you get to play devil's advocate."

"They're both still working?" Adam asked.

"Yes. She's a mental health counselor, and he's a trial attorney."

"Interesting," Adam said. "I thought that name Bob Ballard rang a bell." He laid the piece of paper on his desk. "Call Westwood and set up a meeting with him first thing tomorrow morning," he instructed his office manager. "He's due a report and I'm due an explanation."

"Concerning Bob Ballard?" she asked.

"Concerning the entire case."

———

"Well, what did you find out?" Westwood eagerly asked from across the desk.

Adam picked a slip of paper from his shirt pocket and handed it to him. "Here's Staci Carew's current address and phone number. She now lives in the Tampa area and goes by the name Staci Ballard, having married Bob Ballard, a prominent local attorney, in case you didn't know. They've been married over forty years. They have two grown daughters who are also attorneys. Staci herself works as a mental health counselor."

Westwood stared at the slip of paper. "Anything else?" he asked in a hesitant manner.

Adam paused before answering. "Yes, there is something else, something you already know."

A longer, second pause ensued. "That she had a twin sister?" Westwood asked hesitantly.

"Yes, and something else you failed to tell me."

Westwood again looked down at the slip of paper as if the answer was written on it. "The bridge incident?" he said.

Adam nodded. "The question is, why didn't you tell me about this before I got started?"

His client shook his head as though reluctant to spell it out.

"Okay, I'll go first," Adam said, annoyed with the stalling. "After learning of the incident, I got a hold of the official sheriff's report. It essentially stated her sister Kati was killed as the result of an accidental fall from a Withlacoochee abandoned bridge while bridge jumping. Several questions came to mind following a reading of the report and out of curiosity, I decided to take a trip out to the bridge for a first-hand look at the accident site. In doing so, I was puzzled by some of the circumstances. First, why would Kati go bridge jumping alone. It seemed like something a young girl would do with friends. Secondly, how did a gymnast like Kati, an accomplished performer on the balance beam, manage to lose her balance and accidentally fall from the bridge? While there, I measured the width of the bridge railing's surface. It measured four inches, the same as the width of a balance beam, Kati's specialty, which led me to speculate she may have been practicing her routine on the railing. Performing under pressure, as her former coach explained to me, is the key to success. What better way to prepare for pressure than doing your routine on a bridge railing high above a river? Thirdly, and this relates to what I intimated before, why would you hold back on telling me of the incident?"

Westwood continued to sit silently, apparently listening to the debate raging in his head.

"Kati Carew was not alone on that bridge, was she?" Adam asked directly.

Westwood let out a deep breath. The story within the story was about to pour forth, Adam figured.

"She was known as the backflip girl," Westwood began. "Like you say, an accomplished gymnast. 'What do you want to be when you grow up?' is a question I could never answer nor could most of the kids we hung around with. Kati could, however. She wanted to be a gymnast, simple as that. You were also right in saying she was on the bridge to practice her routine in a high-pressure situation. It was one of the reasons she invited Staci and me to join her there. Performing in front of us added another layer of pressure, especially since Staci viewed her sister as a bitter rival for reasons I will touch on later, if you care to hear."

"Oh, I care to hear," Adam said, "but first let me ask, did you drive to the bridge in separate cars?"

"Yes, I was using my parents' car to drive Staci there and Kati was using her parents' car.

"Staci was not aware her sister would be there. Kati's invitation to her was issued through me. I felt if I told Staci, she wouldn't agree to come. As it was, Staci felt she was going on a bridge outing with me alone. I saw it as an opportunity to help mend that hard feelings she held toward her sister.

"Needless to say, I will never forget the scene and what transpired on that day. Kati was already limbering up when we arrived. After a strained greeting between her and her sister, she finished her warm-up exercises and immediately went about her business, lining up alongside the railing for her mount as Staci and I stood by watching. In a single leap, she landed on it feather soft, like a bird on a tree limb. My heart went to my throat watching her. The sun was shining directly upon her like a spotlight and I don't mind saying she looked beautiful. She performed a few front flips, followed by some twists and turns, before lining up for her final series of rapid moves, one back flip, followed by a second back flip, followed by a third, the last one using no hands.

"I don't claim to be an expert. My sole knowledge of the sport comes from having watched it on the Olympic telecasts over the years. However, I don't believe I've seen anything in my lifetime as beautiful and challenging as what she did that day.

"And then in an instant it turned into a tragedy," Westwood continued. "As Kati stood tall with her arms raised high in a kind of triumphant final pose, her sister, in an unthinkable, inexplicable, reckless act, reached out and shoved her from behind, causing her to lose her footing. In an instant, she landed hard, scissor style, on the railing, before tilting sharply left off it. She desperately tried to grab hold of the railing, but it was already out of her reach. She then tumbled head first, off the bridge. As I rushed to the railing to see if I could help her, I heard a sickening thud and was sure it was her head hitting a support. On reaching the railing, I looked over and saw her hit the water. I realized seconds later she must have been knocked unconscious when I saw her body floating down the river. I turned to scramble off the bridge and down the embankment to get to her when I heard Staci shout, 'Roland...no!' I stopped in my tracks. 'What do you mean 'no,' I shouted back, stunned by her reaction.

"'Don't you see? They'll blame you and me,' she said in earnest. 'Think about it. Our future lives are at stake!'

"I was dumbfounded. 'She's your sister, Staci, and right now her life is at stake,' I yelled in return.

"'Yes, she's my sister and that's exactly why you should listen to me. There's nothing we can do now. Didn't you see her body floating face down? She's gone. We now have to think of our futures,' she said, repeating her point. 'Do you want to throw yours away, Roland?' She was speaking in such a calm voice that I began to feel she was the reasonable one. After all, it was her sister. Her view should take priority over mine. 'Come on, let's go,' she said in a more commanding tone and I followed, as if I was looking for an excuse to cut and run. To think there was even the slightest possibility we might have been able to save her sister's life haunts me to this day."

Westwood paused, tears welling in his eyes, his composure collapsing. His past had caught up with him, exacting a heavy toll.

Adam waited a few moments before asking his next question, allowing him time to regain control of his mental state. "So off to the military you went, never to see her again," he said, taking his client's mind off the bridge.

Westwood nodded.

"I'll ask again. Why did you want a private investigator for this job?"

"Because I was hoping for this result. I know it sounds ridiculous, but I was looking for someone who would discover the truth on his own to assure me I hadn't lost my mind over the years. My doctor tells me I'm demonstrating signs of dementia. I've been having problems recalling recent events or recognizing people and places. Funny thing is, my long-term memory seems to be better than the short term one. I guess the long-term one is locked in and the last to go. Nevertheless, that's why I wanted someone to discover my hidden past and discover Staci's as well. Someone who would verify what went down and give me direction."

"Give you direction as to what to do next?"

Westwood again nodded.

"The direction you take is your decision, Roland. It all depends on what you're seeking. Justice? Revenge? Sympathy? Understanding? If it's absolution you're looking for, seek out a priest."

He shook his head in dejection. "Say it was justice for Kati I was looking for. What are the chances of finding it?"

"An accident by definition involves an unintentional element. So, I'll ask you. What was Staci's intent, or as the law wants to know, was there malice aforethought?"

"Premeditation?"

"Yes."

Westwood looked to the ceiling and clasped his hands under his chin, as if in deep thought. "That's a tough one. Who knows what was going on inside her head? Malice unquestionably was present, but to what extent I can't say for sure. What I can say for sure is that it wasn't an accident. On the other hand, I feel confident in saying it wasn't a planned murder, if that makes any sense. After all, she wasn't aware Kati would be there."

"Then you're getting into the various definitions of voluntary and involuntary manslaughter with lots of gray areas there. The intent element is the key in all of them. It would take a prosecutor to sort it all out. It would also take proof, of course, which in this case is circumstantial, excepting your testimony. Also, there is the matter of your culpability, which you need to consider. Staci's intent in shoving her sister off the bridge may be in question, but there is no question as to the intent of you two to cover up the incident."

"At this stage, I don't care about my culpability or the jeopardy it puts me in. As for Staci's intent, it probably falls within one of those gray areas you mentioned."

"It would help if you could explain their relationship, warts and all," Adam said.

"To begin with, they were not identical twins, nor were they alike in their personalities, despite both of them being on the cheer-leading squad. Staci definitely fit the image of the cheerleader, cute, bubbly, and a social magnet. She was captain of the team and ran with a large circle of friends. Kati, on the other hand was a quiet, unassuming girl and generally not interested in fostering friendships."

"Why then was she on the cheer-leading squad?"

"Staci told me the gym teacher who was coach of the team recruited her. There was an empty slot on the team and since she had the looks and talent, the coach felt there was no sense wasting time trying to find someone else."

"You said they were bitter rivals. Can you explain what led them to become so?"

Westwood mulled the question over for a moment. "As I mentioned, Kati was the individualist who wanted to travel her own path, which meant devoting all her free time to gymnastics. Conversely, Staci was part of the school's established social circle, the quintessential cheerleader who fed off her friendships. Ironically, it was their cheerleading experience that spurred the rivalry between the two. Staci may have been the captain of the team, but she was not the athlete Kati was. She was unable to perform the floor exercises, the cartwheels, backflips, handstands, or any other skill with nearly the proficiency Kati could. This led Staci into believing her sister was trying to upstage her and she let her know. It was the main reason Kati quit the team and went her own way. She felt the friction it was causing with her sister was not worth it."

"This occurred after Staci had given up on gymnastics?"

"Yes. The rivalry resumed *in absentia*, you could say, when Kati's gymnastics career took off. Articles began to appear in the local papers about the girl who was making a name for herself in the gymnastics world. She was winning regional competitions and out of nowhere had become a candidate to make the national team. You would think a sister would be proud of a sibling's success but not so with Staci. I don't know why she harbored such deep resentment. Perhaps it was simply petty jealousy. Whatever it was, it was clear it had become toxic."

"Clear in what way?"

"Through the off-hand comments she would make to me and others."

"Like?"

"Like Kati's growing a big head from all the attention she's getting. She needs to fall on her butt to deflate it."

"How did their parents view all of this? Were they aware of the level of hostility between the two?"

"No, they were not. You have to realize all of the enmity was coming from Staci and she kept it below the surface. Kati, for the most part, ignored it. Since they were not openly fighting like cats and dogs, their parents were mostly unaware of the hostility. When spats did occur, they attributed it to normal sibling rivalry. Staci said as much to me. To give you an idea of her mindset, she once made a point of telling me she was born a half hour before her sister, as if it was reason for Kati to defer to her as the big sister."

"Yet, you didn't let it affect your opinion of Staci, whom you continued to court."

"No, it did not affect my opinion at the time. Staci always displayed her better side when she was with me. The occasional outbursts toward her sister, I also mistakenly attributed to normal sibling rivalry."

"At some point it had to have risen above petty jealousy," Adam pointed out. "So far, I agree, it doesn't sound like anything other than your normal sibling rivalry."

"Oh, I can tell you exactly when it turned toxic," Westwood said, as if saving the best insight for last. "It was when Staci was dumped by Paul Madden, the football captain she had been dating. It riled her no end. I'll be honest and admit it was the reason she took up with me. I was a college guy and for a high school girl to date a college guy was considered a step up in class back in those days. She saw it as a way to get back at him. If that was the end of it, then things might have settled down. However, to make matters worse, Madden later took up with Kati who suddenly had become a prize catch what with her beauty, talent, and notoriety. Staci, of course, blamed her sister for the breakup which could not have been further from the truth. I tried to convince her of this but she wasn't buying it." Westwood threw his hands in the air. "There you have it, the classic high school soap opera."

"With one big exception, most high school soap operas don't end in a homicide," Adam retorted. "Staci's anger was firmly rooted by the time of the bridge incident, would you say?"

"Yes, anger, envy, and resentment, whichever, she was consumed by it."

Adam leaned back in his chair and folded his arms. "Mr. Westwood, it's your call as to Staci's intent and culpability. I'm convinced you think it was much more than a fit of pique that caused her to react the way she did, now that you look back on it as an adult. If so, the real reason for your decision to hire me becomes clear. You're looking to right a wrong, not reconnect with a lost love. Correct?"

"Correct," he said, exhaling a deep breath.

From the corner of his eye, Adam caught sight of Tamra crossing the room with a piece of paper in hand. Something important, he reckoned. She rarely interrupted a conference of his unless it was so. She handed him the note, along with her own message. "I thought you might want to see this."

Adam took the note, read it, and laid it on his desk. "It looks as though this case has already risen to a new level," he said. "Attorney Robert Ballard has demanded a meeting with me."

"How did he become aware of this?" Westwood asked anxiously.

Adam boiled down the possibilities quickly. It wouldn't have been Rick Cooper or Glen Martin, he was sure, nor Anna Korlov. "It likely was the alumni spokesperson at Staci's old school who assisted me in my search," he concluded. "She no doubt alerted Staci, who in turn informed her husband there was someone snooping into her past, someone by the name of Adam Fraley."

"What now?" Westwood asked.

"Let's hear what Ballard has to say before we proceed."

"His getting involved, what does it tell you?"

"It suggests, Mr. and Mrs. Ballard are prepared to go to great lengths to keep the lid on this, which may say something about the truth of it all."

CHAPTER FIVE

Bᴏʙ Bᴀʟʟᴀʀᴅ sᴀᴜɴᴛᴇʀᴇᴅ ɪɴᴛᴏ Aᴅᴀᴍ Fʀᴀʟᴇʏ Pʀɪᴠᴀᴛᴇ Investigations, Inc., sporting a black pinstripe suit, light blue shirt, red bow tie, and thick white hair swept to the nape of his neck. Rimless glasses provided a clear view of his beady brown eyes. He wasted no time in seeking out Adam. "Are you Fraley?" he asked upon arrival at his desk.

"Guilty," Adam said, motioning him to have a seat.

"I'd like to talk in private," Ballard said, nodding toward Tamra.

Adam was about to say the session would continue "as is" when Tamra spoke up.

"I have an errand to run," she said, excusing herself.

Ballard turned half his attention back on Adam, the other half on the room. "Let me give you a little advice," he said in a condescending tone. "A one-room office is not functional, even for a private eye. The least you could do is install some partitions to allow a degree of privacy. You want your office to give off a good first impression. Right now, it looks like your standard low-budget motel reception room what with all the fake indoor plants and rented furniture. And what's with the wooden file cabinets? I'm surprised you don't have rotary phones or roll-top desks, not to mention typewriters. This is the nineties, not the forties, or are you trying to pass yourself off as a modern-day Philip Marlowe? For God's sake, man, this kind of environment will have your clients nodding off to sleep faster than a Sunday sermon."

"Nodding off into the big sleep, you mean," Adam said through a grin.

The reference having bypassed him, Ballard ended his rubbernecking and took a seat. "Well, Mr. Fraley, I understand you've been trying to dig up dirt on my wife," he said, switching to an accusatory voice.

"I'm not sure I would put it in those terms, but yes, I was checking on some information for a client."

"For what client?" he asked directly.

"You, of all people, should know that is privileged information," Adam responded, certain he never mentioned Westwood's name to the alumni lady.

"Tell me, Fraley, don't you ever get tired of being nosy?"

"Only when I'm sitting in the back of a rented van on a hot day watching some guy do yard work for hours on end."

Ballard carefully removed his glasses, slipped a handkerchief from his inside coat pocket and wiped them clean, a mocking smile forming on his porcelain face. It was the kind of smile Adam's old boss once described to him as the "animal smile."

"You see a wolverine, or a badger, or any other wild animal flash a smile and you run the other way," Peterson said. "They're baring their teeth for reasons other than to strike up a friendship. And don't give me that lovable dolphin stuff. That smile is permanently fixed on their face. They'd just as soon take a bite out of you." Peterson hadn't stopped there. "Did you know the advancement of civilization can be measured by the evolution of the human smile? Yep, the first homo sapiens was the first to smile. I figure he was trying to impress some female of the species with a new facial feature and it worked, so others followed in line, ultimately developing it into an attractive human feature."

Ballard, however, shelved his smile in favor of a scowl. "Okay, I'll clue you in," he snorted in response to Adam's deflection. "His name is Roland Westwood."

He either got it from the cops or better yet from his wife, Adam reckoned.

"Do you have a wife, Fraley?" Ballard asked in a civilized manner.

"I don't believe so," Adam said in the flip manner he hated to hear from others.

"Well, if you did, you would understand just how protective a devoted husband can be."

"Protective against what?"

"That's a question you already have the answer to," he said.

"Must be something sensitive for it to bring you all the way down here," Adam said, sticking the needle in a little deeper. "I'll tell you what. Why don't we start over now that you've failed in your attempt at a hostile takeover of this office? What is it I can do for you?"

Ballard stood up, placed the palms of his hands on the desk, and leaned forward, locking his eyes on Adam's. "I'll tell you what you can do. You can lay the hell off my wife or else this little operation of yours will be buried in lawsuits up to your neck," he growled, his face flushing into a crimson fury.

"Speaking of necks, Mr. Ballard, you might want to check your bow tie. It's clocking in at 2:40."

Ballard straightened himself but not his tie. "Very cute, Fraley." He turned and stamped toward the door, crossing in front of Tamra, who had returned from her errand. He paused to cast a nasty glare her way before turning his attention back to Adam. "Keep this up, Fraley, and you and your piece of eye candy here could find yourselves standing in the unemployment line before long."

Adam shoved his chair back from his desk and rose to his feet, prepared to extend the war of words, when Tamra raised her hand, signaling him to end it.

Ballard turned and left.

"Caught the end of your exchange," his office manager said, settling into her desk. "Nice parting."

"Another attorney who thinks winning through intimidation is a strategy," Adam said. "By the way, how are we coming along with the digital conversion of the files?"

"We're getting there. It won't be long before we can chuck the cabinets, though I would be tempted to keep them just to annoy him."

"You enjoyed seeing him riled up, did you?" Adam asked, as if he also took delight in it.

"I had a hunch I'd better get back fast. I sensed an altercation coming and thought a peacemaker might be needed. It's a good thing he wasn't wearing a regular tie. He might have tried to hang you from the ceiling with it, senior citizen though he may be."

"A bit of bravado on his part is all," Adam said. "I don't take anything from it."

"I take something from it," Tamra said, adopting a serious vein.

"Oh, yeah, what?"

"It goes back to a lesson I learned in an ethics class," she said, swinging her chair around to face his. "For example, suppose there's this guy who is a rare book dealer. One day he is invited over to dinner by a neighbor and his wife. While there, he notices an old bookcase tucked in the corner of their rec room. Out of curiosity, he takes a minute to browse the books. Among them are several valuable first editions of modern classics. The homeowner is not a rare book dealer nor is he aware of their monetary value. The dealer knows if he offers him a small sum of money for the entire collection, there is a good chance the neighbor will accept the offer, unaware of their value but wanting to be neighborly. The dealer decides it isn't the ethical thing to do and decides not to make an offer. Two weeks later, the dealer notices the neighbor is having a garage sale and decides to check it out. Sure enough, loaded in a large container is the book collection with a note attached to the top reading "Take all for $25." The dealer immediately pays the twenty-five dollars and takes off with the books. Was that an ethical thing to do?"

"You tell me what the difference is in the two situations and what it has to do with this case," he said.

"The difference is the neighbor put a price tag on the collection the second time around. It may not have been representative of its worth, but in the dealer's eye, it was the neighbor's responsibility to determine the real worth before putting a price on it," Tamra explained. "What does that have to do with this case you ask? Well, Mr. Ballard just put up the real price tag on the case, the continued solvency of the business. Now it's up to you and Mr. Westwood to decide whether it's worth it."

———

"Mr. Westwood, Adam Fraley here. I'm calling to let you know I had that visit from Bob Ballard this morning."

"Oh, yeah? He warned you to back off?"

"Yes, in no uncertain terms."

"Do you feel this case is worth pursuing any further?"

"That's your call, Mr. Westwood."

"What's the downside?"

"The downside from the legal standpoint is the time lapse and lack of hard evidence. This could easily evolve into a 'he said-she said' case, which gets us nowhere. The other uncertainty is whether an actual crime was committed. The district attorney's office would have to make that determination."

There was a pause on the other end of the line. "I'm not sure what good it does to pursue it any further," Westwood said, his resolve wavering.

"What good does it do?" Adam posed. "I'll tell you what good it does. It does a conscience good. It does a justice system good. It does a legacy good. In fact, it does all mankind good if you want to get grand about it."

"Does it do you any good?" Westwood asked.

"Aside from earning a few bucks, yes, it gives me the personal satisfaction of sticking it to Ballard. I know that's not the professional thing to say, but, hey, I don't care for the guy. He's someone who goes out of his way to invite dislike." Adam waited for a response. "Well, what'll it be?"

"I've thought this over—I don't know how many times—and I've decided I sure as hell don't want to carry this to my grave. For Kati's sake and to a lesser extent mine, the truth needs to be told. It can't die with me, which it undoubtedly will, unless I follow through on my original intent. Tell me, what's the next step?"

"The next step is to take the case to the sheriff's department to see if they will conduct a review of it based on new testimony. I'll contact Rick Cooper, a sheriff's department deputy I met on my previous trip up there, to request a hearing."

"Let's do it," Westwood said. "I would have liked to have met with Staci first, but that no longer appears to be an option, considering all that's transpired in the meantime."

"I will set up a meeting with Cooper," he said in closing. "And, Mr. Westwood, I have a feeling that face to face meeting you're wanting with Staci may still come to pass one way or the other."

———

"It would be nice to know what sort of person Staci Ballard is... whether she's a clone of her husband or not." Adam said to his office manager, following his conversation with Westwood.

"Why don't I find out," she replied

"How do you propose to do that? We don't have a lot of time tracking down her present and former associates to dig up their opinions of her."

"I'll go the direct route. I'll book a therapy session with her. She has no idea who I am."

"Therapy for what?"

"A work-related issue."

"Work related? Care to explain?"

"It's privileged information, Adam. The issue is irrelevant to the case, anyway. You said you would like to know what kind of person she is. Why don't you let me find out?"

"How much is this going to cost us?"

"It will be an hour session at the most. A hundred dollars or so I'm thinking."

Adam pondered the idea for a moment. Tamra was a good judge of character, no question about that. Maybe it was worth a shot. "Go for it," he said. "How soon do you think you can get in for an appointment?"

"Soon enough. There are always appointments being canceled or time slots being set aside for emergency visits. I'll see if I can get placed on standby status. The issue does need resolving as quickly as possible," she said, tweaking Adam's curiosity further.

Later in the day, following lunch, Tamra informed him she was booked for a therapy session with Staci Ballard first thing in the morning.

———

Staci Ballard's office was located in a converted red brick house in the historical Hyde Park section of Tampa. The two-story structure housed several other professional offices, including an accounting firm, an investment advisory service, a realty group, and a mortgage broker. Ballard's office was located on the second floor of the structure and looked less like an office than a living room. It featured an Indian rug centered over an oak hardwood floor. Several large oil paintings were aligned along beige colored walls. A wide window stretching from the floor to the ceiling provided a clear view of the surrounding environs. Adjacent to the window was a bookshelf bordered by potted indoor plants. Two tan velour armchairs were positioned across from a companion couch. Staci Ballard occupied one of the armchairs, Tamra the other.

"You are an office manager?" Ballard asked, reading from a background form Tamra had filled out prior to the session. The form did not ask for names other than her own. As decreed at the top of the document, the privacy of clients would not be violated.

In keeping with the spirit of the decree, she had already made up her mind to pay with a personal check to avoid a connection with Adam Fraley Private Investigations.

"May I ask, what kind of a firm do you work for?"

"A security firm."

Ballard spoke in a soft tone befitting the surrounding decor. She was impressive in her appearance, Tamra noted. Her gray tweed suit, ashen hair, and perfectly carved features gave her a statuesque appearance. She couldn't help but wonder how many hours a week Ballard devoted to maintaining the look.

Ballard crossed her legs and glanced down at the clipboard resting in her lap. "What is it that brings you here?" she asked.

"I'll be very direct," Tamra said. "I have a bad case of being in love with my boss."

"Okay," Ballard said, drawing out the word, as though taken aback by the suddenness and nakedness of the declaration. "Can you elaborate on why that is a problem?"

"The problem is, I'd like for my feelings to be reciprocated. At the same time, I fully understand in a workplace environment, especially in a supervisor-subordinate arrangement, that is not always the case nor should it be."

"The personal and the professional are obviously colliding," Ballard said, intimating it was a subject that came up often in the course of her workday.

"Yes, and it's making it difficult for me to function. On the one hand, I love my job. On the other, I love him, too much it seems."

"How many employees in your office?"

"Two, he and me."

"So, you have a close environment within which to operate. Is he married?"

"No, though he does have a daughter."

"From a previous marriage?"

"Through adoption. He's never been married, nor have I."

"Does he have a girlfriend or significant other?"

"There's another woman from out of state he sees on occasion. I'm not sure how serious their relationship is."

"Serious enough for him to travel there?"

"Yes, on occasion."

"And for her to travel here?"

"Yes."

"How long have you worked for him?"

"Five years."

"Does he recognize your feelings toward him?"

"He views my feelings toward him as those of a competent and loyal employee. He's not aware of any romantic feelings I harbor toward him."

"If he is unaware of your feelings, then we can say right off the top this does not meet the definition of an unrequited love, for the simple reason it has yet to reach that stage," Ballard said, uncrossing her legs. "How long have you held these feelings?"

"Nearly the entire length of my employment, save for the opening few months."

"I take it you haven't dropped any hints."

"Correct."

Ballard paused briefly to collect her thoughts. "The likelihood, Tamra, is that your relationship with your boss is not going to change unless a 'change agent' appears."

"Meaning what?"

"An outside party signals to him your romantic interest. Or you could act as the change agent by inviting him over for dinner, or to the theater, or to a ball game, or to whatever. Something to bring you together outside the workplace where the rules of conduct are less defined. Do you have any common interests?"

"Reading and travel," she cited off the top of her head.

"Perhaps you could plan something around one of those."

"Like a book club for two," Tamra said, attempting to inject a bit of humor into a topic that was beginning to give her a headache.

Ballard set aside her clipboard, as she did Tamra's attempt at humor. "As a point of interest, if the situation was reversed, as it is in most cases, there would be far less hesitation. Men are much more likely to act on their impulses, particularly when operating in close quarters. That may say something for your boss."

Tamra nodded her agreement.

"As I see it," the therapist continued, "you have the choice of continuing as is or, like I suggested, changing the dynamic by taking the relationship to a personal level. As I'm sure you are aware, the latter raises the risks, including the possibility of personal rejection, which could end, not only the chance of a personal relationship, but the existing professional one as well."

"It may not be my preference, of course, but I can see myself continuing as is, though there have been times when I thought it would be best to resign and take another job."

"That usually occurs when one of the parties is married and wishes to avoid an affair. Out of sight, out of mind is a viable strategy if adhered to. Unfortunately, even that circumstance has the potential of escalating into something more serious, if the emotions cannot be controlled."

"I assure you I have no intention of ending up as a psycho bitch, if that's what you're suggesting," Tamra said with a beaming smile.

Ballard retrieved her clipboard to again check her notes.

"Oh, my God!" Tamra shouted to herself on spotting through the window a man getting out of his car in the parking lot and strolling toward the building's entrance. Bob Ballard!

Okay…that's it…time for me to hit the panic button.

"Excuse me, but do you have a restroom I could use?" she asked.

The blank look on Ballard's face reflected the unexpectedness of the request. "Yes, at the foot of the stairs, turn to your right. You will see it."

Tamra hustled out of the room and down the stairs, taking them two at a time, like she would do when she had to go really bad. To think, as a precaution she had anonymously called his office secretary beforehand to verify he would be in for the day and was told yes. Obviously, that was not the case.

Cursing her luck, she found the bathroom, and no sooner had she entered it than she heard the front door of the building open. She quickly locked the door and listened for footsteps. She heard them go up the stairs and stop. A knock on the door and seconds later voices filtered down the stairwell, fueling her anxiety.

"What the hell do I do now?" she asked the bathroom walls. For one thing she could immediately take off, make a mad dash to her car and flee the situation. Without paying? That surely would prompt a search for her, which would lead eventually to Adam Fraley Private Investigations and Adam murdering her on the spot in a textbook example of voluntary manslaughter. "Your honor," she could hear him saying in the aftermath. "There was no premeditation on my part to the slaying and dismembering of my office manager. It was simply a visceral reaction to the dumb-ass act of stiffing her therapist out of a payment while purportedly on a mission for my firm."

She could still hear the voices coming from the top of the stairs. Staci undoubtedly was telling her husband she was in the middle of a session and was waiting for her client to return from a bathroom break. What he was saying in return was anyone's guess. With her ear to the door, she reached back and flushed the toilet to let the world know the room was occupied, forgetting it was also signaling she was close to finishing her business.

"Oh, for God's sake," she snapped, realizing moments later the toilet was continuing to run. She flipped open the closed lid and discovered the bowl clogged. She frantically flapped the flush handle, oblivious to the notion she may be making the situation worse. She watched the water begin its relentless swirl to the top edge of the bowl. She looked for a plunger but there was none. As panic set in, images of brooms lugging buckets of water from a scene in Disney's Fantasia danced in her head. It was not beyond her imagination to envision the door bursting open and a cascade of water gushing through it, carrying her into the foyer where Bob and Staci Ballard would find her lying face up at the foot of the stairs.

"Okay...okay...calm down," she admonished herself. Fixing a toilet may not be a skill of hers but past experience had not left her completely bereft of bathroom basics. She hurriedly felt for and found the shutoff valve, at once closing it to halt the spiraling water before a drop fell to the floor. She closed the toilet lid and with the calm came the sound of footsteps descending the stairs. She waited until they dissipated, whereupon she completed her bathroom break and returned to the therapy room.

"Sorry for the interruption," Tamra said politely, retaking her seat in the armchair.

"That's quite all right," the therapist said. "My husband filled the void. He stopped by to discuss dinner plans."

"Regarding my present situation, I don't want to make it seem like I'm asking for suggestions on how to establish a personal relationship with my boss. I know you are not in that business," Tamra said. "I suppose what I'm after is a method to cope with the circumstance, other than to cut and run."

"One approach to the problem some people take, and one I definitely do not recommend, is what I call the 'focusing on faults' approach. Frequently in these situations, one party, in a desperate attempt to cope with their insecurity, will concentrate on the deficiencies of the person they are enamored of in order to cast them in a negative light, eventually to the point of losing interest in them," Ballard explained. "Unfortunately, this can turn a bittersweet relationship into a sour one, with all the attending consequences."

"My boss has his share of faults, but none to dwell on," Tamra responded.

"Can you give me an example of one?" Ballard asked, pressing the point.

Tamra pondered the question. "Well, I would say he has a sense of humor almost to a fault. He can find it in most anything, with the exception of personal tragedy. For instance, he would find my being here something to poke fun at."

"He would not find it tragic in a personal sense?"

"Of course not."

Ballard cautiously nodded her understanding. "Back to your previous statement, You are right in saying it is not within my purview to dispense strategies for forging personal relationships, especially in a business atmosphere. Like I said, you appear to have two options. Either go along as is and cope with the mental stress as best you can, or, as you say, cut and run. In the latter instance, there is always the chance he may see you in a different light once you are no longer an employee of his."

"Can't you give me just one strategy?" Tamra joshed.

"Women have their ways," came her perfunctory answer, as though she believed in none of them.

"I suppose things could be worse. I know a woman who lost her longtime boyfriend to her sister. Now that's a cause for distress!" Tamra said and waited for a reaction, but none was forthcoming. "Well, you have been a big help," she followed. "There's really not much more to be said. It's clear I have a decision to make and I can't expect you to make it for me. Again, thank you for seeing me on such short notice." She retrieved her checkbook from her purse and wrote out a payment of a hundred bucks and left, satisfied she had gained a peek into the core of Staci Ballard.

———

"How would you describe her?" Adam asked.

"Polished, professional, but far from personable," Tamra answered. "There's a dullness to her eyes. Perhaps living with that hubby of hers for all these years has turned her to stone."

"Or she had her game face on," Adam suggested.

"She appears to lead a very ordered life. Her office is in order, her line of questioning is in order, her clothes are in order, and her hair is in order. What else can I say? She is an ordered woman. At one point in the session, I had the opportunity to draw a reference to a friend of mine who lost a boyfriend to her sister, which I thought might throw her off script."

"Oh yeah. Her reaction?"

"None to speak of, though her eyes betrayed her calm exterior. For an instant there, they came alive. It touched a nerve all right."

"Anything else?"

"That's about it," she said, deciding to leave out an account of the

Bob Ballard episode, since nothing came of it, and why worry him further?

"She bought your problem-at-work ruse?"

"Oh, there was nothing to buy. It wasn't a ruse."

Adam cocked an eye her way.

"Remember? The issue is confidential. I can't go further into it."

"How do you expect the issue to get solved without my knowing what the issue is?" he asked.

She shrugged. "Maybe because I'm one of the few who in certain situations believes in procrastination as a problem-solving strategy. This is one of those situations."

"Answer me this then, do you like your job?"

"I love my job. I love everything about it."

"Except for?"

"You'll have to trust me on this one, Adam. I can tell you this much. Even if it doesn't get resolved, it's not going to lead to the downfall of the business. I repeat, I love my job."

Adam sighed his frustration away and smiled his approval. "That's all I need to know. Now I can go home happy," he said, leaving the issue hanging in the air.

CHAPTER SIX

HOME FOR ADAM AND HIS DAUGHTER WAS HIS FORMER BOSS'S old place, one Pete Peterson had put up for sale when he retired to the Keys. However, Peterson was unable to sell it due to a down housing market. When he lowered his price out of necessity, Adam jumped at it. Located in a mid-town complex comprised entirely of cream-colored villas with orange tile roofing, it was conveniently located to Noelle's school and his downtown office.

As it happened, the discussion he and his daughter were having this evening on their ride home from softball practice centered on his and Tamra's decision to lodge a formal protest regarding Noelle's suspension. His daughter was not at all convinced it was worth pursuing, which she later revealed at the dinner table.

"Why go to all the trouble?" she asked, following a hearty meal of spaghetti and Italian sausage he had cooked up. "Our coach said I would only be out for one game. I'll be back in the lineup in time for the first playoff game."

"As I explained to you, baseball managers, football coaches, basketball coaches-all coaches—are arguing for the next close call, knowing they were already going to lose the one they were presently engaged in, despite the histrionics they put on display. It's a way of gaining leverage."

"You're not the coach," she countered.

"The principle is the same for whoever is doing the arguing, whether it's on the field or off."

"Didn't you sign the parent's code of conduct on how to behave at games?"

"That's a promise not to make a scene during a game. Filing a formal protest with the league office regarding the breaking of a rule is not making a scene. It's going through the proper channels."

"Sometimes I wish I was a boy, then I'd have a chance to grow up and make a living playing baseball."

"It's not that easy, Noelle, even for the select few who make it to the majors," he pointed out. "Which reminds me, did I ever tell you the story of the legendary Sam Fullerton?"

"You tell me very few stories anymore."

"Well, here's one for you. Sam Fullerton was a can't-miss pitching prospect who made it to the big leagues as a starter. However, the guy never came close to the stardom that once was expected of him by people in the know."

"Who were the people in the know?" Noelle asked.

"Scouts, managers, and player development people. Anyway, he ended up bouncing around the league for the better part of eight years before landing in the bullpen of one of the bottom-feeding teams. At first, the excitement and challenges of putting down a late-inning rally made life in the bullpen livable for Sam and eased his transition from starter to reliever, but as the months and season passed, the challenges were becoming fewer and farther between and, as a result, the excitement faded. However, there came a special challenge toward the end of his career in a winner-take-all final contest. Of course, there was no way Sam with his three-and-ten record or his cellar-dwelling team could come out of this game a winner. No, the only drama remaining for them on that day rested in the fortunes of the opposing team who was involved in a three-way scramble for the league title. It was the kind of storybook finish league officials dream of, a story that would draw an overflow crowd to the stadium on the day of the final game."

Adam took a swig of water from his dinner glass before continuing. "The situation was this," he said. "Sam's team was leading nine to eight. There were two out in the bottom of the ninth and the home team had runners at first and second with two out when Sam got the call to put out the fire. However, Sam knew there was another element to the story, for it was his intent on entering the contest to not only throw the ball but the game itself, to make a gift of it to their opponent."

"Why was he going to do that?" Noelle interjected.

"Money. He had convinced himself that was the name of the game. Grab as much as you can before you are no longer able to grab anymore. He had had plenty of time to think things through while sitting out there in the bullpen during those long hot days in the sun. It gave him plenty of time to reflect on the dwindling opportunities left in his career, on a wife and two kids he had to support. Given the right opportunity he would not hesitate to secure their future. Well, the opportunity came during a break in the schedule when an old friend of his turned gambler talked him into a simple transaction. It meant several thousand dollars, payable upon delivery."

"How was he going to throw the game?" his daughter asked.

Adam held the palm of his hand face out. "Hold on now. I'm about to tell you."

"When he took the mound, his manager and catcher were there to greet him. 'Don't give him anything good to hit,' his manager said. 'We still have third base open,' meaning a walk would not be disastrous. Sam nodded his agreement to the manager who handed him the game ball. He then took his allotted warm-up pitches. He was a big southpaw with a big motion...big windup, big kick, and big follow through.

"Having completed his preliminary pitches, Sam toed the rubber, glanced at the runners and unloaded a fastball that caught the outside corner of the plate for a called strike. 'Probably got all their hopes up a little with that one,' he thought. 'Better throw him a few bad ones.

Got to set him up nice for the payoff pitch. Maybe go to a three-one count. That way he knows I got to come down the middle. No, better make it a two-one count. Might let one get away on a three-one and walk him. Yeah, wouldn't that be something,' he thought. 'Then they would lift me for a right-handed reliever to face the next guy.'

"So, with his game plan finalized, Sam proceeded to deliver two more fast balls well wide of the strike zone, the last one nearly bypassing his catcher, causing Sam a moment of panic and the home crowd to growl their disapproval.

"'Well, here we are,' Sam said to himself. 'Now he knows I gotta come in with a pitch. How about a hanging curve ball, a batter's best friend? Just hang one out over the plate. Let him get under it and stick it in the wind. Blowing pretty towards right. He'll never miss it-couldn't.'

Adam scooted his chair back from the dinner table, stood up, and assumed the pitcher's stance to act out what was to transpire on the field. "Again, Sam toed the rubber and leaned in for the sign. He shook off two, nodded an okay at the third. Another check of the runners, and he delivered the payoff pitch.

"Sam tracked the flight of the ball from his follow-through position, feet planted wide apart, eyes glued to the plate, watched as the hitter stepped deep into the batter's box with his right foot while in the same fluid motion releasing the bat from its cocked position, driving it forward until it met the pitch midway across the plate. Contact! Crack!

"A screamer, a rocket shot, a blue streak, a frozen rope line drive bore down on a startled Sam. He moved his glove to shield his face and in the same instant felt a soft tug in the webbing of his glove followed by a collective groan from the direction of the stands. 'Caught it!' he shouted to himself. 'Drop it! Drop it!'

"Too late. Sam looked up from his glove and saw the plate umpire with an upraised arm signaling an out and his catcher with an extended one closing in for congratulations."

Adam sat back down in his chair and folded his arms across his full belly in satisfaction at the telling of the tale. "There then is the story of Sam Fullerton," he said to his daughter.

"What's the moral of the story? Don't bet on baseball? We all know that," she said, seemingly unimpressed with the presentation.

"No, not the moral, The lesson," Adam patiently replied.

"Okay, what's the lesson?"

"The lesson is you can defeat your opponent and you can defeat yourself, but you can never defeat the game. If you try, it will always come back and bite you in the butt."

With that, Noelle stretched out a lock of her light brown hair for him to see. "When do I get to cut this?"

"When you're twenty-five, the same age you can start dating."

Noelle tossed him a dumbfounded look. "Get serious. I'm almost twelve, you know. Bobby Taylor asked me the other day after class if I'd like to go get a pizza with him someday."

"And you said?"

"'I'll give it some thought.'"

"Were those your exact words?"

"Yes. Why?"

"How do you think it came across to him?"

"I don't know. It got the point across."

"The point being?"

"I wasn't sure I wanted to go get a pizza with him, so I told him I would give it some thought. What's so bad about that?"

"What if you went and asked a boy to go get a pizza with you and he said he would give it some thought. How would that make you feel?"

She shrugged her shoulders and threw out her hands. "What should I have said?"

"You could have given him an age appropriate answer, like I'll have to check with my father first."

She again hunched her shoulders.

"You should choose your words carefully, Noelle. Make sure they convey your intent, okay?"

"Okay," she said and resumed pulling at her long locks. "Did I tell you our coach said I'd probably raise my batting average twenty points if I had hair that wasn't getting in my face," she said, continuing to tug at her locks.

It was Adam's turn to hurl his daughter a disbelieving look. "Then wrap it up."

"That's what older women do," she countered. "You need to listen to a female's point of view more often."

"More than I already do? As things stand now, I listen to Tamra all day and you at night."

Noelle giggled in reaction. "Tamra's going to teach me how to cook nutritious meals," she said.

"Great," he responded, gathering up the empty plates and dumping them into the sink. "Have you been complaining to her about my cooking?"

"No, but it wouldn't hurt me to start learning," she said, joining him in cleaning the dishes. "Don't you think Tamra is very pretty?" she asked, following a brief silence.

Oh no, here we go again, Adam thought. "Yes," he answered in a matter-of-fact manner.

"She thinks you're handsome."

Adam cast a sideways glance at his daughter, prompting her to cup her mouth with a hand to stifle a chuckle.

"Don't you have some homework to do?" he said, taking over the dish washing duties.

"She thinks you're handsome," he repeated to himself. Whereupon followed the attending questions swirling in his head. Did Noelle, in all her eagerness to play cupid, let slip the workplace issue occupying his office manager's mind? If so, was Staci Ballard now more privy to an office undercurrent he was not even aware of? Surely, Tamra did not name names in the therapy session, so what was he concerned about? Wary was he of having his own feelings exposed? Hell, he should have hired a guy in the first place as his office manager, he concluded, prompting a final question. Who was he fooling?

CHAPTER SEVEN

ADAM SAT AT HIS DESK, PONDERING WHETHER THERE WAS ANY meaning to the fact three of his major cases in recent years centered on bridge incidents, all leading to fatalities. Two of them, the Tampa Bay Sunshine Skyway Bridge and the Colorado Royal Gorge Bridge events involved suicides while the issues surrounding the Withlacoochee abandoned bridge matter were still up in the air. The symbolism of it? Well, a bridge does connote a crossing over. Thus, a decision to end a life in a suicidal manner supposedly could symbolize the same, he reasoned. A bridge also represents hope, a better place awaiting on the other side for those seeking to reach a new destination or overcome an obstacle, such as Kati Carew's determination to perform a back handspring in a highly pressurized situation.

"Did you get your message," Tamra asked from across the room, ending his meandering reflections.

"What message?"

"The one laying on your desk, the one from the Colorado cop."

"You mean from Carlita Perez," he said, signaling his annoyance at her impersonal reference.

He found the message tucked beneath another note. "She's

attending a conference over in Orlando and wants to know if I'm free on Saturday. If so, she'll drop over," he said aloud, inviting a reaction.

Tamra sat with an easy smile on her face. "Well, are you?"

"Noelle does have another softball practice scheduled," he said, unable to disguise the plea in his voice.

"I'll take her, Adam," she said. "I wouldn't want you to miss out spending a day with Carlita."

"Are you sure?" he asked. "It's not like I haven't imposed on you enough already."

"No problem," she said, the smile still clinging to her face.

The phone rang, saving Adam from further unease.

"It's for you," Tamra said. "Anna Korlov."

"Oh, yeah?" he said and punched in on the line. "Adam Fraley here."

"Mr. Fraley, this is Anna Korlov, Kati Carew's former coach, if you recall," she said in her distinct accent.

"I certainly do," he said.

"You may also recall the old facility I told you about, the one up the road we now use as a storage unit."

"Yes, I remember you making reference to it."

"Well, we were cleaning some old lockers out of there yesterday, something we should have done long ago, and discovered one of them had belonged to Kati. I don't know what, if anything, is in it. The lock has not been removed. We were about to toss the whole thing out but then I thought it might be something you'd be interested in seeing."

"Definitely," he replied. "Do you recall if investigators checked it following her death?"

"I'm sure they didn't. It's a small locker, tucked away among a lot of others. I doubt it crossed anyone's mind, including mine, to check the possibility there was one of hers still around."

"Listen we're planning to come up Thursday for an afternoon meeting at the sheriff's department. Could we stop by your old facility, say about ten in the morning to take a look at it?"

"Yes, I could meet you at the front entrance. As I said, it's approximately a mile north of our present facility. It's one of those corrugated metal structures that were popular back in the forties. You can't miss it."

———

Anna Korlov was there to meet them at the entrance to her storage facility. Following a brief introduction to Roland Westwood, they trailed the retired coach into the building and through a maze of gymnastics equipment to a room in the back crammed full of old olive-green lockers, shrouded in a haze of musty air.

"I've been wanting to get rid of these for some time but have never got around to it. I guess you could call me a pack rat," she said. "Kati's locker is down this row," she added, motioning for them to follow.

The two followed her through a narrow aisle to the last locker in the row. "This is it," she said. "You can still see Kati's name stenciled at the top."

Adam noted the padlock on the door. "I take it you no longer have a key to the lock?"

"Lord knows where it could have ended up," she replied.

Adam turned to Westwood. "Here, take my keys and grab the crowbar out of my truck."

"Do you think it is okay to do this?" Korlov asked hesitantly. "We won't be breaking any law, will we?"

"Not after this much time has passed," Adam said. "No family member has come to claim it, right?"

"Not that I know of."

"By now, it is considered unclaimed property. It's yours to do with as you please," he said, reasonably sure of his off-the-cuff interpretation. He glanced about the cramped facility. "This is where Kati got her start. I imagine it looked far different back then."

"Yes, it did," she replied, "but, believe it or not, it was far less functional than it is today."

"This building?" he asked, curious as to why.

"Simple as there was no air conditioning. This place was like a sweat shop, which made it much more difficult for students to perform. Sweaty bodies, especially sweaty hands, caused problems for the gymnasts, particularly on apparatus like the high bars and balance beams. We put up some big fans and opened all the windows and doors, which helped a bit, but still our athletes operated at a distinct disadvantage when it came to preparation. It was no mystery at the time why the cold climate nations dominated the sport. It was not just gymnastics. All indoor sports in Florida suffered in comparison to the outdoor."

Adam recalled his grandfather's tales of life before the introduction of air conditioning to the state. How normal it was for people to wake up in a sweat, and not from fever or fear. How everyone would frequently sleep on the porch and drive their cars with the windows down. Florida was like every other sleepy southern state before "AC" was introduced, he would point out. All it took was the arrival of the room air conditioner to spur the population movement southward.

Westwood returned with the keys and the crowbar. Pocketing the keys, Adam took the crowbar in hand and snapped the lock with a couple of downward thrusts. Inside the locker he discovered an array of vintage athletic gear, including athletic tape and wrap, a gym bag, a couple of towels, cans of disinfectant and deodorizer, and an empty water bottle. Hanging on a hook was a light jacket. Adam lifted it and held it out for Korlov to see.

"Yes, many of the girls had warm-up jackets. They'd wear them inside and outside on those rare days when the temperatures cooled."

Adam returned the jacket to the hook. In doing so, he felt something hard inside one of its pockets. He lifted the item from its pouch and held it up to the light. "It's a pocket planner," Korlov said. "We advised the girls to carry them, so they could maintain a record of their workouts and competitions."

Adam fingered through the notebook, its pages yellowed by time. "Roland, could you run back to my truck and check my glove compartment. There should be a copy of the incident report in it," he said, once again handing him the keys.

"Anything interesting?" Korlov asked.

"Nothing thus far," he said. However, it's going to take time to comb through it carefully.

He was still perusing through the record book when Westwood returned with the report. He checked it for the date of the incident. "June 18, 1943. Does that sound right, Roland?"

"Yes, it was a Friday morning."

Adam hurriedly turned to the date in the planner. Scribbled inside a note box was the following: "Meet Staci and Roland at the W. bridge–9:00 a.m." He held up the opened page for the two to see. "I'd say this is a very productive trip thus far," he said, pocketing the planner.

———

Adam resumed his perusal of Kati Carew's notebook as he, Westwood, and Rick Cooper, the architect of the meeting that was about to commence, sat around an elongated conference room table, waiting for the arrival of the sheriff Scott Hayden. The furnishings for the room were plain and spare, the colors muted from the walls to the windows. A shaft of sunlight streaming through half-opened blinds helped brighten the room.

The sheriff, a man with thick, winter-white hair, ruddy complexion, time-chiseled face, and cast-iron frame brought along a cohort, a twenty-something woman with close-cropped black hair, thin face, and cat's eyes. She was introduced as Detective Marian Costello.

Following introductions, the sheriff immediately launched into the business at hand. "Okay, we've read the original report, now you tell us your version of the events," he said to Westwood whose fatigued eyes betrayed a weariness of the path he was traveling.

Westwood told his story as he had told it to Adam, right up to the point where Kati gloriously completed her back-handspring routine on the bridge railing and stood triumphantly with her arms raised high, at which point he paused in his presentation. Tears again welled in his eyes, turning them to a milky blue, and bringing a palpable unease to the proceeding.

"This is the point where Staci shoved her sister?" the sheriff asked, ending the pause.

Westwood recovered his composure enough to say, "Yes, this is when Staci shoved her sister off the bridge," he stated, a statement that spurred an exchange of glances between the participants.

"Mr. Westwood," the sheriff said, looking him directly in the eye. "The story you are telling us now is the true one, not the one you gave the investigators in the original report. Correct?"

"Correct."

"Why now and not then," the sheriff followed.

"I was afraid," he said simply.

"Of what?"

"Of everything, Staci, the law, my family, even my future."

"And you are going to stick to the truth this time around?"

"After seeing Kati's locker this morning and the personal feelings it reawakened in me, I am all the more convinced the truth needs to come out," he said firmly.

The sheriff leaned back in his chair. "Kati shouted 'Don't' to her sister the moment she was shoved?"

"Yes. She hardly had time to get the entire word out before she fell."

"Why would Staci react in such a way?" Costello asked in a soft voice. "On the surface, it obviously amounts to a severe overreaction. Wouldn't you agree?"

"Looking back, I no doubt misjudged the depth of her hostility toward her sister. The truth is, I liked Staci. She was a completely different person when not around Kati."

"Did her sister feel the same way about her?" Costello asked.

"No, she harbored no ill will toward Staci, as far as I could tell."

"Explain the boyfriend issue," Adam said. "It may help explain the depth of Staci's hostility."

Westwood repeated what he had earlier discussed with Adam regarding Paul Madden's dumping her in favor of Kati and the deep resentment that ensued. He also elaborated on the other rivalries between the two, including the cheerleading competition. "I know they may seem like normal high school conflicts, but I can attest they were bitter to the bone in Staci's case."

"To clarify a couple of points," Costello said. "When you say Madden dumped her in favor of Kati, does that mean Kati was out to steal his affections? It doesn't seem to fit her character the way you describe it."

"I stand corrected," Westwood said. "Kati did not steal Madden's affections. There was an interim between Madden dumping Staci and his taking up with her sister. In Staci's mind, however, there was a connection."

"How long an interim?" Costello asked.

"Three to four months, I'd say," Westwood responded.

"Did you ever speak to Paul Madden about this?"

"No. I felt it was none of my business, plus he was not someone I spoke to often. He was nothing more than an acquaintance."

"As far as the other rivalries, they were also viewed as such only by Staci?" Costello asked.

"That is correct. I should have made that clear."

"Is this Paul Madden still around?" the sheriff asked.

"I checked," Adam said. "He recently passed away after being confined to a nursing home with Alzheimer's."

Hayden glanced down at the notes he had been compiling. "Technically, this is not a cold case though the challenges are similar or even greater since a judgment has already been rendered. The key, as with any cold case, is the gathering of new evidence. The only thing we have in this regard is the recanting of original testimony by a former college student who now claims he witnessed his girlfriend shove her sister off the bridge in a fit of rage. Is that it?"

"We did uncover a new piece of evidence this morning," Adam interjected, holding up the notebook he had brought along. "This is Kati's planner in which she clearly states her intention to meet her sister and Mr. Westwood on the abandoned bridge on the morning of the incident."

"Where did you come up with that?" the sheriff asked.

"From an old gym locker of hers."

"Okay, good, that lends credence to the argument she intended to be there, not that she actually was there, however," the sheriff pointed out. "For that we still only have Mr. Westwood's testimony."

"What was her intent in meeting you there," Costello asked of Westwood.

"Her coach said that for her to reach her potential as a world class athlete, she would have to learn how to perform in high pressure situations. She believed performing her back-handspring routine on a bridge railing in front of her sister and me would help her in this regard," Westwood said.

"The bridge routine was not the coach's idea, was it?"

"No, it was Kati's."

"Who issued the invitation to the bridge?" Cooper asked.

"Kati, but only through me. Her sister had no idea what the get-together on the bridge was about, other than a routine outing with me."

"Kati, on the other hand, expected her there, right?" Cooper asked.

"That speaks volumes about how Kati viewed her relationship with her sister," Costello said.

"How so?" asked the sheriff.

"Normally, you consider a sister as supportive of your athletic challenges, not a person hostile enough to wish you defeat. For Kati to view the bridge scenario as a high-pressure situation underscores her recognition of the existing hostility toward her. Ironically, her flawless routine ultimately served to prove how right she was. For her effort, what was she awarded? A death without dignity by her sister."

Hayden combed back an unruly lock of hair with his fingers while collecting his thoughts. "This is a rare situation we're dealing with here, folks. A young girl accused of killing her sister. In all my years of law enforcement, I don't recall it happening. Doesn't mean it can't happen, but what it does mean is that it will take a lot of convincing to persuade others it did."

The sheriff turned to Costello. "Ever hear of such a thing?"

She shook her head. "No, never heard of such a case. I've heard of the term for it, though. *Sororicide.* If I recall right, it's a combination of the Medieval Latin words *sopor*, meaning sister, and *caedere*, meaning to strike or kill, thus the act of killing one's sister."

"Cooper, how about you?"

"None I can recall."

"Fraley?"

"Goneril poisoned her sister Regan to death in King Lear," Adam said, his remark drawing blank stares and immediate embarrassment for him.

"It comes from a Shakespeare play," Costello explained, coming to Adam's rescue. "One sister kills another in a struggle for power. Come to think of it, there is a parallel that can be drawn to this case. Goneril, the dominant sister, is angered by the thought Regan might lure Edmund, a co-conspirator of hers, away from her circle of influence in much the same way Staci, the once dominate sister, is angered by Kati's taking up with Madden, her former boyfriend. As you say, rivalries can turn cruel, though rarely to this level. Those between twins can turn especially intense. The question thus becomes, what was Staci's intent in shoving her sister from the bridge and was it premeditated?"

"I don't consider it premeditated," Westwood said. "I feel she acted on the spur of the moment."

"She may have acted on the spur of the moment, but she was the cause of her sister's death, if what you say is true," the sheriff responded, to which Westwood nodded his agreement.

"We can run this by the district attorney to determine exactly what level of crime we are talking about, given the circumstances," Hayden said. "In the meantime, we are going to invite Staci–what's her last name now?"

"Ballard," Adam answered.

"We'll ask Staci Ballard to come in for questioning."

"Do you want us to attend?" Adam asked, meaning he and Westwood.

"Not for the initial meeting. Down the line, probably so, if this case goes forward. A defendant has the right to face her accuser."

"Her husband is a noted trial attorney," Adam pointed out.

"So? Isn't everyone related to an attorney nowadays?" Hayden quipped. "I anticipate he'll come along with her. We'll see. Meanwhile, keep in mind a lawyer can't stand in the way of an investigation, even if he's the spouse of the suspect and representing her."

"It would be interesting to know how much of this incident, if any, she has shared with her husband," Costello said. "How long have they been married?"

"Forty-five years," Adam responded. "To address your point, I'm sure the sharing started the moment they got wind of my snooping around. As to whether she broached the topic with him from the very beginning of their marriage, she may well have related how her sister died, sticking to the official version."

"It'd be interesting to know what how much detail of the incident she may have felt obligated to share with him," Costello followed.

"It'll all come out in the wash," the sheriff stated with confidence.

Hayden picked up his notes and slipped them into his briefcase. "As I said earlier, this case is similar to a cold case in its challenges. Obviously, we're looking across a great chasm of time. Witnesses are no longer available, victims' relationships change, and friends are no longer friends. Nonetheless, the time interval can also work in our favor as evidence once considered lost or undiscovered turns up unexpectedly. Your assignment is to keep digging up those buried memories. Who knows? Nuggets of truth may be buried with them."

"'Time shall unfold what plighted cunning hide,'" Costello said, drawing another stare from the sheriff. "Cordelia…King Lear," she added, ending the session.

"Where was Kati buried?" Adam asked, directing his pickup home, following the meeting with the sheriff.

"In a church cemetery. Why?" Westwood asked back.

"On occasion, if the circumstances invite it, I like to take a personal interest in certain cases of mine. This is one of them. That might not seem professional, but I find that it can be an extra motivating factor for me to finding out the truth," Adam explained. "Is the cemetery far from here?"

"Maybe three or four miles at the most."

"Show me the way."

They zigzagged a few rural roads until they ended up completely off the beaten path, eventually coming upon a small, white clapboard church ringed by a wrought iron fence. A signboard in front of the church simply identified it as St. Joseph's Church. No other information was given.

Adam pulled his pickup to a stop alongside the fence. "Is this place still in operation?" he asked.

"I don't believe so," Westwood said. "If I recall right, there's a new St. Joseph's Church located further down the road that took the place of this one."

The cemetery was to the rear of the church. There were no more than two dozen grave sites, Adam estimated at first sight. Whether planned or not, each was placed next to one of the many large oak trees that graced the grounds. The oaks stood like sentries aside the graves. "It doesn't appear to have reached complete abandonment status," he observed. "It looks as though someone is at least providing minimal maintenance."

"My guess is the diocese is providing it," Westwood said. "They no doubt would like to sell the property but probably are at a loss as to what to do with the buried."

"It won't be long before it's deemed to be standing in the way of progress," Adam cynically observed. "I can see an apartment complex or strip mall one day standing here. Or maybe a golf course," he added, drawing a grin from Westwood.

The two strolled past the burial sites, Westwood leading the way.

"She was laid to rest over here," he said, stepping toward a plot adjacent to one of the trees. A gray marble headstone bore a simple inscription.

In loving memory of
Katherine (Kati) Carew
Beloved daughter and sister
May 19, 1925 - June 18, 1943

The two stood in respectful silence, listening to the wind rustling through the oaks, their limbs draped with thick strands of Spanish moss stretching nearly to the ground. Overhead, passing puffs of clouds, swept along by a tropical breeze, shuttered sunlight and shadow on the scene below.

"You say it's a motivating factor for you to take this case personally. Why so?" Westwood asked.

"I take it personally when someone is victimized by the legal system, which I am linked to by profession, even if it's the result of a simple sin of omission on the part of those who failed to get things right in the first place. Kati was a victim twice over, by her sister and by those in authority. I don't want there to be a third time."

"Nor do I," Westwood said.

"What was it like the day of the burial?" Adam asked, his eyes fixed to the grave.

"Weather-wise, much like today," Westwood said, momentarily lifting his gaze to the sky. "Lots of friends, family, and classmates showed up to express their condolences. I could not help but wonder if the sorrow expressed by the persons paying their respect was greater than hers."

"By hers, you mean Staci?"

"Yes."

"You still think that?"

"I would hope over the years the memories of better times would have softened her view toward her sister. I don't need to tell you that memories are the lifeblood of the elderly. They can sustain us for the remainder of our lives. Unfortunately, all it takes is an especially rotten one to spoil the bunch."

"You knew her sister well, Roland. What do you feel would be her cry from the grave?"

"I'm not sure there would even be one. If so, it would not be one of vengeance. I can tell you that. It was not in her nature. If anything, it would be a cry for the truth. I don't think she, or anyone else, wants to leave this world with an incomplete story of their life being told, especially one with a false ending."

Adam lifted his eyes from the grave to view the surrounding area. "Her parents are not buried here?"

"No, they passed away long after the cemetery was closed."

"What kind of people were they?"

"Just that, kind, gentle, humble. They ran a mom-and-pop general store over near San Antonio. To make matters worse for them, the store was robbed right after Kati was killed. I think it was around five thousand bucks they lost. Lots of money in those days."

"They were in the store at the time?"

"It was an overnight job. The only employee they had was a girl by the name of Betty Ann Carver. She was part time and served as assistant manager."

"Did you know her?"

"Yes. She was a local girl who I would see out and about and at the store. As a matter of fact, she was one of the people I contacted in my initial search for Staci. Working at the store, she knew both of the sisters. She's someone you might want to interview also."

"Do you recall where she lives now?"

"Not off the top of my head, but I believe I still have her address and phone number on me." Westwood fumbled through his billfold, pulled out a crumpled slip of paper, and handed it to Adam who stuck it in his pocket.

Turning his attention back to the grave, Adam noticed a wilted floral bouquet resting at the foot of the headstone. Someone had visited the site in the not too distant past, he reckoned. Nonetheless, he avoided the temptation to ask Westwood if the bouquet was of his doing.

Suddenly, a young wood stork from one of the many nearby

marshes crashed the scene, descending through the trees and alighting atop the gravestone. Slowly and carefully, the feathered intruder walked the length of the marker, stepping gingerly with its elongated, dark gray legs. Midway across it stopped, flapped its black and white wings and hopped several about faces and side steps. Having completed its performance, it stood erect, tilting its head as it pondered the presence of the two onlookers pondering it in return.

"Would you say the width of that headstone is about four inches," Adam asked.

Westwood gave him a puzzled look. "Yeah, I'd say so. Why?"

"Just curious."

The stork finally departed, as did they, taking with them a memory or two.

CHAPTER EIGHT

KAREN COX, SUPERVISOR OF OFFICIALS FOR THE SOUTH Florida Girls Softball League, had the signed parents' behavior form resting in clear view on her desk, as if prepared to reference it at the least provocation, when Adam and Tamra arrived. She was a petite woman with straight, leaf-brown hair cut to the neck, and brown eyes to match. A wane smile clung to her face, disappearing the moment her two visitors took their seats across from her.

"You're Adam, the father of Noelle?"

"Correct."

"And you're Tamra, the...?"

"Watchdog of Noelle," Adam volunteered, drawing perfunctory grins from both women.

Cox nodded, deciding not to pursue the matter of familial connections any further. "I understand you have a complaint you would like to file with the league pertaining to Harlan Weeks, one of our umpires," she said, looking back and forth at the two.

Adam motioned to Tamra. "She'll take it from here," he said.

Tamra presented their case, describing pitch after pitch landing in the dirt before reaching home plate, culminating in Noelle's ejection from the game. To back up her argument, she occasionally showed selected footage of the contest, utilizing the camcorder she had brought along. Altogether, a concise and effective presentation, Adam believed, biased though he was. But was the supervisor of officials listening? Her body language signaled otherwise. Despite the intermittent nods and fake smiles, her eye contact was as disengaged and empty as a scarecrow's. Her body was here but her mind was paying no heed to the argument advanced by his cohort, Adam noted with dismay.

Cox delivered her reply to Tamra, occasionally shifting her eyes to Adam in a manner tantamount to looking over a person's shoulder to the presence of a more important personage, a discourtesy unlikely to go unnoticed by his office manager.

"The first point I make to friends and families of participants in our league is that we are not only a competitive league but a recreational one as well. Fast-pitch softball is not always suitable for those who view it exclusively as a competition. There is also an overarching social benefit to the game. In the end, we don't want people, fans and participants alike, to walk away from a contest thinking they are losers."

"Meaning the point of the game is to participate, not necessarily to win," Tamra countered.

"Again, there is a recreational aspect to the sport that cannot be ignored. The ultimate purpose of our game, after all, is to have fun."

"Some people—no, many people—think winning is fun," Tamra said pointedly.

"Not when it becomes a detriment to the purpose of the game. Taking a called third strike in the dirt unfortunately happens at times. How a parent, player, or coach reacts to bad calls says as much about their character as it does the competence of the man calling the balls and strikes. Calling into question the umpire's judgment based on one plate appearance does not set a good example."

Karen Fox's mind was no longer disengaged from the conversation nor was Tamra about to let her disengage from it again. "First of all, we are not calling his competence into question based on one plate appearance. He was doing it for the entire game. Secondly, we are protesting in the preferred manner recommended by the league, not by shouting obscenities from the grandstand like many do. Are you saying there is nothing wrong with the plate umpire's performance or his reaction to Noelle's restrained response to his calls?"

Cox tossed another quick glance Adam's way, as though to say, 'Can't you shut her up.' "Listen, between you and me, Harlan Weeks, the umpire in question, is a longtime benefactor of the league. There might not even be a league if not for his generosity. Allowing him to umpire games seems a reasonable accommodation in return," she said, laying bare the truth of the matter.

"We are told not to discuss other coaches, players, or parents in front of the children," Tamra shot back, motioning to the parents' behavior form on the desk. "We are told not to put suggestive thoughts in anyone's head like so and so over there is a terrible center fielder. We, definitely, are told not to argue balls and strikes from the stands. Well, just what are we to do when a plate umpire continually and without question calls pitches in the dirt strikes? More importantly, what are you to do?"

Cox's answer was to shrug her shoulders, meaning Harlan Week's standing was above reproach in the eyes of the establishment, despite the visual evidence.

Adam sensed Tamra was ready to play hardball, perhaps threaten to take the tape to the local media as she had suggested to him earlier and let them make a fool of the guy, a ploy he felt could easily spark a sympathetic public backlash in favor of the elderly ump. How would the owner of Adam Fraley Private Investigations and his daughter look then? Regrettably, the business angle could not be ignored. When the mud started to fly, it would stick on anything or anyone involved.

"How about this for a compromise?" Adam said, breaking from his spectator status. "The suspension of Noelle is immediately lifted in time for her to participate in the playoffs and the matter of Harlan Week's competence is left for you and the board of directors to decide at their next board meeting? Unless, of course, you are willing to risk it becoming a matter for the local media."

Cox thought a moment and jumped at it. "Sounds like a reasonable approach," she said, lifting the parent's behavior form from her desk and sliding it into a drawer. "Consider Noelle officially back in the game."

———

Tamra was still in a fighting mood back at the office. "You let her off the hook," she lamented, shoving her handbag with the camcorder in it back into her desk drawer

"We got what we came for…Noelle back on the field," he said.

"What if Harlan Weeks is back behind the plate for her next game?"

"I expect he'll be assigned to another game. We'll see."

Tamra opened up a cup of chocolate ice cream she had purchased on the ride back from the meeting. She was in need of some comfort food, she freely admitted, to settle her stomach. A few bites into it, however, she set the spoon aside and pressed her fingertips to her brow.

"You having a brain freeze?" Adam asked.

She nodded, slowly releasing her fingers.

"Those things remind me of a hemorrhoid problem I had a few years ago," he said, ignoring social graces.

Tamra had resumed eating her ice cream but immediately set it aside again. "Adam, I'm really not in the mood to hear about your hemorrhoid problem, especially after sitting through the hemorrhoid inducing discussion we had with Ms. Cox."

"It's related to the discussion," he said, sticking with the thought. "Anyway, I took my problem to the doctor who supposedly was a specialist in the elimination of hemorrhoids by freezing them."

His office manager was not about to be distracted from her treat, scooping up the chocolate delight with deliberate speed while ignoring the ramblings of her boss.

"I go in for the appointment and he gets me in the proper prostrate position for his treatment, which by the way he claimed was the quickest and surest method to rid a patient of the damn things. He then takes this device off the table that I swear looked like a sawed-off Star Wars sword fitted with an illuminated stick of dry ice for a blade. He shoves it up me and straight into purgatory I go. The closest feeling I can compare it to is the brain freeze, except it's not like having an icicle jammed up your nose into the roof of your mouth. No, it's the experience of having your whole body overwhelmed by a numbing wave of pain. Afterward, while the doctor was putting away his instrument, I was still stepping to and fro, like I was performing some kind of rumba or samba, trying to find something in his office solid enough to lean against until the shock wave passed."

Tamra had her elbows back on her desk and her fingertips back to her brow in a futile attempt to conceal her laughter.

"I did get rid of the hemorrhoids, you'll be pleased to know," he said, when her phone rang putting an end to the mirth.

No sooner was Tamra on the phone than Adam grabbed a second incoming call. "Fraley Private Investigations."

"Mr. Fraley, Rick Cooper here. The Assistant District Attorney Carl Stevens has scheduled a one o'clock meeting for tomorrow afternoon in his office in Dade City to hear the results of our interview with Staci Carew. The purpose of the meeting is to determine whether we should proceed with the case. He would like for you and Mr. Westwood to attend."

"We'll be there," Adam said. "Can you give me a heads up as to what her response was to the inquiry?"

"The sheriff thinks it best if the D. A. hears it at the same time you and Mr. Westwood do. Sorry."

"Fair enough," Adam said. "Tomorrow it will be."

———

"Bottom line, they're sticking to the original report," Cooper said from his seat at the D. A.'s conference table.

"To clarify, by 'they' you mean Staci and her husband," the sheriff said.

"Yes, Staci and her husband who was serving as her attorney," Cooper said.

"Did she deny the allegation directly or through her husband?" Adam asked.

"I asked her directly and she denied it directly." Costello said. "Nearly all other questions were fielded by her husband."

"Did you believe her?" the Assistant D. A. asked.

Stevens, a lanky man in the early years of middle age, sat erect in his chair, hands folded in front of him like a sitting judge patiently waiting for a case to be made. He was clad in an off-white suit, lime green shirt and white tie. His light tan, soft brown eyes, and matted down flaxen hair contributed to the composed countenance he presented.

"The fact she let him do almost all of the talking says a lot to me," Costello answered. "If I was innocent, I would be shouting it from the mountain tops, husband be damned."

"First, you have to find a mountain in Florida," the sheriff cracked.

"Okay, on top of a soap box," she retorted. "In any case, she appeared to me to be following advice of counsel and not her conscience."

"What about you, Mr. Cooper?" Stevens asked.

"I agree. Her eyes were saying one thing, her voice another."

"Other than denying Mr. Westwood's claim, did she have any explanation for his making the charge?" Stevens asked.

"Her husband said it was likely a dementia issue," Cooper answered.

Stevens turned to Westwood. "You have a dementia issue?"

"Nothing that would be considered out of the ordinary for a man my age," he said.

A nice dodge, Adam thought.

Stevens looked at him with hesitation. "Nothing to cloud your judgment?"

"No, my judgment is intact."

"Are you willing to take a lie detector test?" the sheriff asked.

"Yes," he said firmly.

"For our benefit or for the court?" Stevens asked the sheriff. "Remember, in Florida both parties must agree to it beforehand if the results are to be entered into the record. It's a risky step."

"Since our case depends almost exclusively on the testimony of Mr. Westwood, I say we go for it," the sheriff stated. "We have to buttress what we've got."

Stevens looked to Westwood. "You're willing then," he reiterated

"I'm willing," he said, repeating his resolve.

"Okay, I'll get in touch with Ballard to see if he's prepared to roll the dice for his client," Stevens said. "If he's as convinced about his wife's innocence as he purports to show, he could well go for it."

"I have a few questions for Mr. Westwood regarding the relationship between Kati and Staci and how it became lethal," Costello proffered.

"Yes, I'd be interested in hearing this matter explored, particularly if we are to establish a clear motive," Stevens said. "Have at it."

"Let me preface this by saying I don't believe the relationship between Kati and Staci in the end was a sibling rivalry as commonly defined. Rather, it was a sibling betrayal in Staci's eyes, a much more insidious situation at work and a rare one among sisters."

Costello must be the department's de facto in-house shrink, Adam surmised. It certainly made sense to have someone like her on board given the necessity of determining motives, particularly in a case predicated on finding one.

"With this in mind, Mr. Westwood." she continued. "I'll lay these elements out there that are intrinsic to a sibling betrayal and you tell us if they apply in this particular case. You don't have to give us specific examples for now, only your acknowledgment they were at play. Okay?"

Westwood nodded his understanding.

"First, sides were taken with rivals."

"Could you explain what you mean by *sides were taken?*" Westwood asked

"For example, in the formation of school cliques, extra-curricular activities, or sporting competitions, did one sister invariably take sides with the rival or rivals of the other."

Westwood thought a moment. "Yes, mostly at Staci's instigation. Kati was not interested in rivalries outside of official athletic competitions."

"False rumors were started or spread."

"Yes," he responded quickly. "Again, mostly on Staci's part."

"Competing for the sole purpose of preventing the other from winning."

Westwood paused in thought. "Yes...homecoming queen competition for example, though Kati, from the beginning, showed no interest in competing."

"Forcing friends and family to take sides."

"Definitely. I was on the receiving end of it from Staci."

"Growing quiet or irritable when forced by circumstances to be around each other."

"That often was the case," he replied. "It was the case on the bridge."

"Staci was the irritable one, Kati the quiet one. Is that how it went?"

"For the most part, yes."

Costello continued with her list. "Constant attempts to one-up the other."

"Again, attempts from one of the sisters in particular," Westwood responded.

Costello looked up from her notes. "You are definite in saying these elements originated almost exclusively with Staci?"

"Yes, but that's not to say Staci didn't have her good side. I can't stress that enough. In all other aspects of her life, including her relations with me or others, except her sister, of course, she was a fine person. Otherwise I wouldn't have considered her for my girlfriend."

"Losing her former boyfriend, Paul Madden, to Kati was that the last straw for her?"

"I wouldn't categorize it as losing a boyfriend to Kati. It wasn't a case of Kati stealing him from her. Staci and he had already broken up some time before. I always had the feeling the Staci and Paul relationship was similar to an arranged marriage. The two were looked upon as the town royalty, societal pressures having pushed them together as a result of them being named homecoming king and queen. That was fine with Staci but not so with Paul, who I believe felt forced into the personal relationship. From what I gathered, Paul's interest in Kati developed later on."

"To Staci's chagrin?"

"Definitely. It also raised in her suspicions that Kati may have harbored secret feelings toward him all along and may have acted on them in some secretive way."

"Did Staci discuss with you her past relationship with Madden?" Costello asked.

"On occasion, often enough to let me know it was a touchy subject with her," Westwood said. "Though she never came right out and said so, I sensed she felt they would someday be getting back together again."

"From the way you describe her, Kati appears to have been a sensitive person. She must have been aware of the effect of her taking up with Madden would have on her sister, despite the interim following the breakup," Costello proffered. "Do you know if she ran it by Staci first?"

"I'm sure she did. At one point in our relationship Staci casually mentioned to me the two were dating. I asked her if she cared and her answer was 'Why should I care.' It was probably the same answer she gave Kati when first told by her of the two's interest in each other."

"She did care, right?" Costello asked.

"Yes, deeply."

"Did you have a romantic interest in Kati?" Costello asked flat out.

"No," he said with a smidgen of conviction.

Costello glanced at the group. "If I may, I'd like to add a few comments before turning the questioning over to you," she said.

"Proceed," Stevens said. "We're listening."

"As I stated, it is critical to draw a distinction between a rivalry and a betrayal. In my opinion it became the latter the moment Madden took up with Kati. It said to Staci there never was a relationship between her and Madden to begin with. It may have been teenage insecurity at work but the reality was Staci felt emotionally raped and eventually took it out on her sister in a spontaneous act of fury."

"Are you justifying Staci's reaction?" the sheriff asked.

"Not justifying, explaining," Costello said. "She felt betrayed. There's a reason Dante placed betrayers in the lowest rung of hell."

Adam was expecting someone to ask who Dante was but thankfully none did.

"Okay, enough of the motive talk for now. Let's get to the crime itself," Stevens said. "Specifically to the scarcity of evidence. What do we presently have? The testimony of an eyewitness that directly contradicts the original report and an entry in a notebook that supports the witness's testimony. Anything else in that notebook to lend support, Mr. Fraley?"

"Nothing thus far. Still combing through it."

"Sheriff, is there anything else your people have come up with?" Stevens asked.

"We've interviewed nearly everyone named in the report who is still around. None were able to add anything new."

Having entertained the group's input, Stevens shifted into his presiding role. "Though I wouldn't call this an altogether convincing case in terms of evidence, I find it sufficiently compelling to request a preliminary hearing, which means we will need to file charges before doing so. The defense no doubt will welcome a preliminary hearing, believing they can have the charges dismissed on insufficient evidence."

"How likely is that?" Westwood asked.

"Given that the beyond-a-reasonable-doubt standard does not

apply in a preliminary hearing, a reasonable amount of evidence will do. The goal of the process is to screen out cases with no or very little merit whatsoever."

"Do you consider what we do have a reasonable amount?" the sheriff asked.

"We have a prime eyewitness who wishes to recant his testimony in a major way. That counts for a lot, especially if the judge considers him believable." Stevens turned to Westwood. "In this regard, the lie detector test plays a significant role."

Westwood nodded his understanding.

"Good. Needless to say, whether we get past a preliminary hearing depends greatly on the results of the test."

"Who administers it?" Adam asked.

"I'll arrange to have an impartial third party conduct it," the sheriff said.

"Ballard will have to agree to the arrangement," Stevens pointed out.

"Right," the sheriff acknowledged.

"Do we have a long wait for the preliminary?" Adam asked.

"Normally, no," Stevens said. "Prelims can be set up within days of the filing of charges. The hearing itself is usually brief, maybe one to two hours. It could be very brief if the judge decides this case is— pardon the pun—water under the bridge. In other words, there is no case."

"There are many reasonable people who would consider it water under the bridge," Costello said. "Why bring it to light?"

The assistant D. A. clasped his hands on the table. "The state has a responsibility to maintain the integrity of the system by correcting injustices, including those committed by the state. Specific to this case, the state has a responsibility to Kati Carew, a girl with a promising future that was taken from her in a reckless manner, which brings us to the possible charges. I've talked this over with the D. A. and we agree Murder One and Two are out given the absence of a clear premeditation. We next considered the manslaughter charges, voluntary and involuntary. Arguments can be made for either.

Though there may have been malice aforethought, it does not necessarily follow this was a premeditated act. It was a rash act, born of malice that led to the death. The perpetrator, Staci in this case, acted with culpable negligence, a wanton disregard for human life. The D. A. and I agree the proper charge is involuntary manslaughter. Does anyone here disagree with this assessment?"

The group exchanged glances with no one voicing disagreement.

"What chance does the D. A. give this case?" Adam asked.

"Not a great chance but he feels it's worth the effort for the reasons I just discussed. One factor in our favor is that the Ballards have already boxed themselves in a corner in one important regard. They've denied on record Staci was on the scene at the time of the incident. The courts do not take kindly to perjury. If Staci repeats her denial under oath and it's proved otherwise, she will be subject to a severe penalty. Much of it depends on how aggressively they pursue the discovery process. Preliminary hearings can come and go quickly. It's common for the discovery process not to run its course until an actual trial is deemed in the works."

"Can I hang on to this for a while longer?" Adam asked, holding up the notebook.

"Yes, but don't lose it," Stevens said. "It does not become official evidence until it is placed in the legal chain of custody."

"What about the statute of limitations relating to perjury in the original investigation?" Adam asked.

"Good question. Perjury in official proceedings that relate to the prosecution of a capital offense has no statute of limitations. However, this case has yet to be determined to meet the definition of a capital offense, which requires that a felony be punishable by death. We are ruling that out with our decision to go for the involuntary manslaughter charge. Nonetheless, if Staci repeats under oath what she stated in the original investigation or recently repeated to Deputy Costello and Deputy Cooper and it is proved false, she is subject to a perjury charge."

"I feel it is important Mr. Westwood is made aware of the risks involved in filing a complaint," Adam said.

"Of course," Stevens replied. "If someone pleads not guilty to criminal charges and the charges are dismissed or no conviction results, the accused party has the option to sue their accuser for malicious prosecution, court fees, punitive damages, and the like. Are you willing to accept the risk?" he asked of Westwood.

Westwood straightened himself in his chair. "I am," he said with firmness.

"Good, so we will proceed with the filing of the involuntary manslaughter charge. In the meantime, keep up your pursuit of evidence."

Westwood will be fulfilling his heart's desire, Adam mused, following the session. The opportunity to meet face to face with his first love of nearly a half century ago might not be in the manner he'd originally envisioned, but it would be a meeting nonetheless.

CHAPTER NINE

_____

Adam dubbed it the mangoes and mangroves day trip. "I decided we would do something Florida-like to celebrate your former stay here," he said from behind the wheel of his pickup.

"From the direction we're headed, you must mean South-Florida-like," the Colorado cop responded from the passenger side.

They were approaching Tampa Bay's majestic Sunshine Skyway Bridge connecting Pinellas and Manatee Counties. The span's soaring cables glistened in the early morning sun, adding an ornate glow to the landmark structure.

"This is where you got your start in the business, right?" Carlita asked halfway across the span.

"Yes, my first case so to speak, thanks to my old boss who gave me free rein to run with it. He could have easily taken it over, considering my inexperience."

"How is Pete?"

"Still enjoying his retirement in the Keys."

"Still mentoring you?"

"As needed, which means frequently."

They were off the bridge, headed directly south on I-75 in moderate traffic.

"Noelle has grown into quite the young lady," she said. "Must be good parenting."

"If not for you, I wouldn't be a parent," he said, acknowledging her role in setting up the adoption.

She had driven over from Orlando to his place at an early hour. Noelle insisted on cooking them breakfast and then insisted on accompanying them on the trip. "Don't you remember, you have softball practice today. Tamra has agreed to take you," he at once said, squelching the idea of her going along. The truth was he could not recall a time when he had been out with Carlita, here or in Colorado, that Noelle had not tagged along. It was as if she was acting as his permanent chaperon, or should he say his matchmaker. One way or the other, there definitely would be no third party on this trip he had decided beforehand.

"It goes without saying Noelle was overjoyed to see you," he said. "You are her lifeline to Colorado."

"I'm so happy for her," Carlita said. "I'm sure her mother would be pleased to know she's in good hands."

Adam flashed a shy grin her way. The woman looked not much different from the first day he saw her several years past. She still possessed the same willowy figure, dark complexion, clear green eyes, and dark brown hair she had tied into a ponytail. For the trip she wore shorts, a t-shirt, sandals, and a wide brimmed hat, which she had tossed into the rear seat.

In the beginning, he doubted a long-distance relationship would work, but over the course of time, the mutual admiration overcame the geographical divide. No matter the occasion, here or there, Carlita was the woman he was always thrilled to see arriving and saddened to see leave. She was a testament to the notion the body first attracts, and the mind subsequently holds or repels. Thus far in the relationship, the holding part of it held fast with minor interruptions. He attributed the resilience of the relationship to a lost art—the handwritten letter.

He recalled the first of them, leaves of paper filled with beautiful handwriting and intimacy of thought. Eventually, they came to mean much more. The seeing and touching of what had become her familiar style of letter stirred a warmth in him before he even read the words.

"Who writes these anymore in the digital age?" he'd asked himself. But that was the point, he soon realized. It was what made them special. The unspoken message in choosing this form was *you mean a lot to me, so I'm setting aside this time to express it.* He tried to follow suit, though his handwriting was largely illegible, even to his own eye. As a result, he took to printing his letters back, which she found to be no less rewarding. "I hope I don't run out of things to say," he wrote early on. "I am a male after all."

"Just talk about your life," she'd written back. "That way I can learn everything about you."

An hour south of the Sunshine Skyway they exited the interstate and drove another half hour west to Pine Island, a large inland island strung between the Southwest Florida barrier islands and the mainland. Pine Island itself was surrounded by a maze of mangrove islands of widely varying shapes and sizes.

"There's a fruit farm operation not too far down this road where we can stop and pick some mangoes," he said.

"Pick or pick up?" she asked.

"Pick–the only way to shop for fruit if the option is available, especially with the mango season well under way."

"Do you have an eye for picking fruit?"

"The question should be do you have the back for it? I once worked on a fruit farm northwest of here for a summer while attending school. My father said it would provide me some good work experience and it did."

"I've heard it's tough work."

"For the first week it's hell until your mind and body adjust to the rhythm of the job. Throwing a spike-tipped ladder up against a tree full of fruit in the proper manner and climbing up it without the ladder tipping over is a skill not easily acquired. There were several times I tipped over and crashed landed on the ground, taking with me several apples I shook loose from branches I was desperately trying to grab hold of to break my fall."

"You were an apple picker?"

"Apples, pears, oranges, mangoes, strawberries—you name it, and for eight hours a day, oftentimes in the rain. The money wasn't great, though it definitely put a strain on the back."

"You were paid by the hour?"

"Some growers paid by the hour, but back then the good pickers could make more money getting paid by the piece. Say you picked sixty quarts of strawberries in less than an hour at twenty-five cents a quart. That's fifteen bucks which was better than most hourly pay rates in those days."

"Did the growers provide overnight accommodations?"

"I commuted from my parents' house. Most of the other workers stayed in accommodations provided by the growers—dorms, converted barns, even in tents."

A small convoy of produce trucks traveling down a dirt access road could be seen off in the distance, trailing a cloud of dust, a confirmation if one was needed that the start of the harvesting season was well under way.

"Is there an art to picking?" she asked.

"You have a basket tied to the front of you like a baby carrier. You climb up and pick. You climb down and empty. Climb up and pick. Climb down and empty. Despite the aches and pains, there is something satisfying about mastering the rhythm of the work. There are also the side benefits of eating healthy and getting a good night's sleep following an exhausting day. All in all, it clears the mind, allowing you to focus on what's important in your life."

"How was the social atmosphere or was there one?"

"Surprisingly, it was good. You met a lot of people from other countries, and what turned out best for me, I met Timmy Whalen."

"And who's Timmy Whalen? I've never heard you mention the name."

"Timmy was a strapping, red-headed, happy-go-lucky guy from New Zealand who led life on the edge. He couldn't wait to see the world, so he decided to experience it by traveling the fruit picking circuit at a young age. Timmy didn't worry about tomorrow, nor did he want to be tied down by responsibility. He was not one for settling down. 'There will be plenty of time for that later on,' he would say. It didn't mean he was irresponsible. If he took on a duty or was assigned one, he would see to it that it was carried out."

"Was he a good worker?"

"He was typical of us younger guys in taking risks in order to fill a bag quickly. For instance, he'd use the top two steps of the ladder—a definite no-no—or even stand on top of it to reach that perfect-looking, forbidden piece of fruit you were warned not to overreach for. Or he'd walk the ladder while still on it to move it a few feet rather than getting off to re-position it."

"He was a ladder acrobat," Carlita said.

"Exactly, and a very productive one."

"You befriended each other?"

"Yes. We hung around together during our off hours, hitting the beach, hiking the nature trails, and fishing the lakes mostly. My parents loved him. We would invite him over for Sunday evening dinners and he would regale us with tales of his world travels."

"You eventually parted ways, though."

"Yes. When the summer ended, I headed back to school and he headed off to Central America for another harvest. We kept in touch for a while but then fell out of touch."

Carlita reached across the front seat and rested a hand on his shoulder. "You should track him down, Adam," she said. "What is it about men that they don't hang on to their friends like women do? Friends are hard to come by."

"I don't know why. Maybe, it's because we've all got that lone cowboy gene buried inside. You're right, though. I should have kept in touch."

She removed her hand from his shoulder. "Do I need to remind you, you are a private investigator? Find him."

"I'll put Tamra on the case, as if she doesn't have enough to do already."

"Well, there's your answer. Lighten her load by hiring him. Surely, you could put his talents to work for you."

Adam considered the thought, deciding that might not be a bad idea at all. The guy was a people person and a fast learner, someone who could adapt to most any situation. His versatility and daring would be a definite plus in a profession often calling for an out-of-the-box approach to problem solving.

Following a quick stop at the fruit farm to pick a small basket of mangoes, they headed to a nearby marina to rent a canoe.

"I'll paddle from the back," he said. "You take the front."

"Don't you mean the bow and the stern," she teased.

"You'll have to excuse my nautical terminology. I was in the air force, not the navy."

The weather gods could not have been more favorable. The dead calm conditions made for a perfect canoe outing. Not so for the sailboats that normally populated Pine Island Sound. In the distance, a yacht lolled in the placid water. Beyond it, a flock of pelicans glided toward the horizon.

Adam took his paddle and shoved the canoe away from the dock and into the open waters. "We'll head straight to that cluster of mangrove islands across the way," he said, dipping his paddle into the mirror-like water to begin the half-mile excursion. Four boat lengths from the dock, they had their paddles in rhythm and the canoe skimming the surface at a steady pace.

Approaching the islands, they were rocked momentarily by heavy swells coming from a passing motor boat but quickly regained their balance.

"Do you see what looks like a tunnel between those mangrove trees ahead?" he called ahead to Carlita.

"Yes, I see it."

"We're going to paddle through it. You might want to tuck your hat between your legs or else you'll risk losing it."

They slowed their speed and entered a thick tangle of vegetation. "Some mangrove tunnels don't allow you enough room to use your paddles, so you grab hold of branches and pull yourself through," he called ahead. "Some tunnels turn out to be dead ends."

"That doesn't seem to be the case with this one," she said, working her paddle carefully between the obstacles.

"No, not this one," he said. "However, if you do have to grab hold of a limb, be careful of the one you choose. There are snakes that blend in nicely with the trees."

"Believe me, if I grab hold of something that slithers, you will know it."

Brushing aside limbs and leaves for fifty feet or so, they came upon an opening to a small cove ringed by mangroves standing ten feet or taller. They lifted their paddles into the boat and surveyed the scene.

"Wow!" Carlita exclaimed. "Is this your hideaway?"

"This is it. I come here, sit in the canoe, read a book, and listen to the birds. It's a sanctuary of sorts," he said. "From the descriptions in your letters, not much different in its peacefulness than your Boulder Creek sanctuary in Colorado, which, by the way, you never took me to."

"Next time...I promise," she said.

They sat quietly, taking it all in when a fish abruptly leaped from the still waters, almost landing on Carlita's hat, before disappearing again below the surface. "What was that?" she asked, startled by the sight.

"A fish."

She threw him a disgusted look.

"A mullet. They are jumpers."

"What makes them jump?"

"A good question with a number of different answers. Some say it's their way of scoping things out—predators, prey, pretty girls, and so on."

Carlita dipped a hand in the water. "So warm," she said, turning to him. "Is it safe to swim in?"

"Safe enough. This is one of the purer coves."

"I have my swimming suit on underneath these," she said, motioning to her outerwear. "Do you mind?"

"Not in the least."

In deference, he shifted his gaze to the surrounding scene as she shed her hat, shorts, t-shirt, and sandals. "All set," she said, drawing his attention back to her, specifically to a yellow bikini that blended nicely with her olive skin.

"Are you going to join me?"

"I can't swim."

"What? You're surrounded by all this South Florida water and you can't swim?"

"Correct," he said in a matter-of-fact manner.

"You never told me you couldn't swim. You should put on one of those life jackets."

"You are my life jacket."

"What if I hit my head on a rock or something? Who's going to come to my rescue?"

"I'll figure something out. Besides, there's small chance of that happening. I know you are an excellent swimmer. In fact, unless you are the one exception, I personally know of no Cuban-American—and I know many of them—who is not a good swimmer. Do you?"

"Not off hand, though there's got to be one or two around," she jested. "I tell you what, Adam, the first thing I'm going to do when we get back to your place is ask your daughter whether you can swim or not. I know I will get the truth from her."

He first looked at her as if he was offended by her doubting him, then let out a chuckle. "You got me," he said, surrendering the truth.

"I knew it!" she said in triumph. "Now why did you tell me you couldn't?"

"For a very selfish reason, Carlita. I would much rather sit here and watch you swim, believe me."

She nodded as if not knowing what to say. "Okay, how do I get out of this thing without tipping it over and dumping you?"

Adam grabbed both sides of the canoe firmly with his hands to steady it. "First thing, stand carefully, keeping your feet on the center line."

Carlita followed instructions.

"Now turn carefully to face the side of the boat, again keeping your feet to the center line."

The canoe rocked a bit from her movement but steadied once she was in position.

"Now what?"

"What you don't do is step on the side of the canoe in the course of your dive. Make like you are on a platform diving board, bend your knees, and dive over the side."

Carlita did as told, propelling herself forward into the air and out of the boat in a makeshift dive. She knifed into the water with nary a splash and disappeared, surfacing seconds later ten yards away. "It worked," she gushed. "You and the canoe are still here."

"Oh, that was the easy part," Adam said with a grin. "The hard part will be getting you back in."

"How do we work that?" she asked, treading water aside the canoe. "There's no shoreline here except for the mangrove roots or else you could beach the boat and I could easily step aboard."

"That would be too easy," he said. "Don't worry. We'll figure it out later. Meantime, I'm going to sit here and enjoy myself."

"If you say so."

She slipped beneath the surface and commenced an underwater swim the length of the cove and back, the serene water allowing Adam a clear view of her back and forth movement. If there was ever a visage to add to the splendor of the cove, it was that of a beautiful woman partaking of its pleasures. It was why he brought her here. Yet, above and beyond her beauty, warmth, and innate goodness was the indebtedness Adam owed to her. She, more than anyone else, was responsible for his receiving the ultimate Christmas gift—his daughter. It was she who guided him through the legal steps to parenthood. Now that he had decided Noelle needed a mother and she had let it be known she wanted one, his search for prospects was officially open with Carlita a logical leading candidate whether she knew it or not.

"I'm ready to come on board," she said a short while later, resting one hand on the canoe's side.

"Okay, do you see that large limb hanging out over the water," he said, pointing to a shaded area across from them.

Carlita swiveled her head around to take a look. "Yes, I see it."

"I'll meet you there."

"No, I'll beat you there," she said, launching into a splash and dash.

He eased the canoe to where she was waiting for him under the limb stretching nearly ten feet out before angling down a couple of feet above the water.

"Can you reach up and grab the end of the limb and shimmy up it a ways with your hands?"

She propelled herself from the water and grabbed hold of the limb with both hands, dripping water as she did. She then edged up the limb until her entire torso was above the surface

"Do I look as awkward as I feel?" she asked.

"Yes, but it's only temporary," he teased, drawing a feigned look of disgust from her.

"Now, if you can do a chin up and bend you knees, I'll maneuver this thing beneath you."

She easily cleared the top of the canoe as Adam slid it beneath her till she was center point above it.

"Good girl. All that police academy training did not go for naught. Now, lower yourself slowly into the canoe."

She did but the moment she let loose of the limb and her feet touched down, a gust of wind came out of nowhere and threw her off balance. Adam reached for her as she tumbled forward, landing in his lap. For a few anxious moments, the canoe rocked violently, though it steadied almost as quickly.

"Well, this certainly wasn't part of the plan," she said, glancing up at him.

"The gods decided to do me a favor," he said.

"Your khakis are soaking wet."

"Terrible, isn't it?"

He still had his right arm wrapped around her mid-section from having broken her fall. He could feel her heart throb from the rush of the moment. Gently, she rested a hand on his forearm. In turn, he took his free hand and turned her face to his. In an instant, his lips were joined to hers and meeting no resistance. All at once the world seemed very far away and insignificant, but for a second burst of wind that sent the canoe rocking again, the kiss might never have run its course, he ventured to think. A nice warm beach on which to stretch out would have been nice, but that was one amenity a mangrove island did not offer.

"Are you conversing with the wind gods again?" she asked.

"They're either jealous or messaging us to get a room," he said, releasing her from his lap.

"Is there a woman in your life, Adam?" she asked, having taken her seat ahead of him in the canoe.

"Yes, the one you helped put there," he answered

She laughed. "You know I'm not talking about your daughter."

"There's you," he said.

"Did you ever consider resettling elsewhere?" she asked.

"You mean, like Colorado?"

"You have said how much you like it there. I know your daughter does. It's her second home."

"And you like Florida and so does Noelle." he countered.

"Maybe we could meet in the middle."

"Sure, in some tiny town where there's no need for a private investigator or cop," he said. "You at one time were a Floridian, Carlita. Did you ever consider returning?"

"If someone offered me a little house in the country surrounded–"

"Please don't say by a white picket fence," he interjected.

"No, by Frangipani trees. There's no fragrance in the world like the one their blooms give off. Perfumes are made of it."

"I agree," he said. "My parents had two of them in our backyard.

Their blooms were very colorful as I recall pink, red, yellow, and white. The only problem is during the off-season they'd lose their foliage. You then end up with a bunch of sticks sticking out of the ground, a real picket fence."

"In that case, I would do a reverse snowbird thing and move to Colorado during the winter season."

"You do know in the Far East Frangipani trees are popular as cemetery plants. They've long been associated with death and dying. It's said their scent is a sign of the coming of a vampire."

"Adam, if the vampire smelled like a Frangipani tree, I would be tempted to let him have his way with me."

Adam looked at her with mock shock.

"But I've always been terrible at giving blood," she quickly added. "I'm sure I'd be able to overcome the temptation. Speaking of places to live." Carlita returned to the subject. "I'm sure you know how fugitives running away from the law, a bad marriage, a scheduled court appearance, or whatever, often end up in the strangest of places, believing no one will ever trace them there. Well, we recently had this one fugitive who went to every length to disguise his intended whereabouts. He started by randomly picking a place to move to by throwing a dart at a map of the United States. He figured the randomness of his selection process would go a long way to eliminate any connection we might make between him and the town he chose. No relatives living there, no girlfriends, no financial transfers, no transportation bookings. No nothing. To further cover his tracks, he also changed his identity and cut off all communication with those who knew him."

"Where was the town?" Adam asked.

"Some small burgh in the far northeast corner of Nebraska."

"How did he get there?"

"Hitchhiked and that is where he got lucky. Some British tourist who happened to be traveling across the country in a van gave him a ride part way. He dropped him off in Lincoln and the guy took a bus the remainder of the way."

"Okay, what's the upshot?" Adam asked.

"The upshot came when we got a search warrant immediately following his disappearance and checked his home in Colorado Springs. What do you know? In his basement, still mounted on his rec room wall, was the map of the United States with the dart still sticking in it. In all his haste and precautions to cover his tracks, he failed to cover the first one."

"Isn't there some kind of award for guys like that. The Darwin Award comes to mind."

"The funny part is after we alerted the highway patrol in Nebraska to his whereabouts, they dispatched two deputies who arrived there before the fugitive did. There was a cafe next to the bus depot and while they were there eating lunch, up pulls the bus with the fugitive on it. The deputies said the look on the guy's face was priceless when they greeted him as he got off."

In time, the shop talk faded, replaced by a stealth silence. It was as though the entire cove and all of its life forms had drifted to sleep, the sole sound that of the water lapping against the canoe. It ended when a woodpecker drummed his presence on a nearby mangrove tree, stealing their attention back. The busy bird hopped up and down from one tree to another in its search for insects before flying off to more fertile hunting grounds.

They spent the remainder of their time munching on mangoes and drying out, all the while watching the comings and goings of a colorful array of seabirds, from blue herons, to white egrets, to a host of others. During one lengthy look-around, they identified eight different species of birds simultaneously perched in the trees, like they were auditioning for an Audubon guide book.

"How did you ever find this place, Adam?" she asked, as they maneuvered the canoe toward the mangrove tunnel, having called it a day.

"I have a fascination with tunnels, the natural kind, not the man-made ones," he said. "To me they represent mystery as well as the promise of refuge from the outside world, so I seek them out. Finding and exploring mangrove island tunnels in particular has become a weekend hobby of mind. Discovering what watery wonder awaits at the end of one is a lure I can't resist."

As they did on their entry, they threaded the tunnel with great care, using their paddles to deflect the impeding branches long enough to escape their backlash. Shortly, they were back on open water and headed for Pine Island, the brightness of the day having dimmed into the shade of the early evening.

"Say goodbye to Carlita's Cove," he said to her as they distanced themselves from the island.

"Carlita's Cove?" she responded.

"Yes, I dubbed it that during one of your underwater laps," he said. "Of course, it's also been known as 'Carol's Cove, Candy's Cove, Crystal's Cove...'"

She took her paddle and skimmed it sharply over the surface of the water, sending a spray of it back into his face. "You'd better hope you don't run out of coves before you run out of women," she cracked.

He liked her a lot, the Colorado cop, with room to like her more. At the end of the day, his feelings toward her had been confirmed. Yes, the challenges of a long-distance relationship were not lost on him. But then, what better way to test the ties necessary to building a bond?

"Daddy, who do you like most? Carlita or Tamra?" his daughter boldly asked later that evening. "I like both."

"I also like both," he said, taking the out she had given him.

CHAPTER TEN

"How confident are you?" Tamra asked, while sorting through the morning mail.

"Not as confident as the Assistant D. A.," Adam answered. "That's not to say he's brimming with confidence himself."

"It doesn't surprise me the way you've been pouring through that notebook for the last week as though it's all you got. Maybe, I should have asked whether you have any confidence in Stevens."

"As a matter of fact, I do. He strikes me as a guy who's interested in what you have to say. He's a listener. Not enough of those in the world."

"Then what are you worried about?"

"I'm worried about our client. Our entire case centers on his testimony and I'm afraid Bob Ballard will chew him up on the stand and make him appear as the victim of an unrequited love who is bent on revenge."

"After all these years?"

"First loves are like first kisses. You don't forget them. At least, that's what I'm told," he said, tossing a grin his office manager's way. He continued his perusal of Kati's planner. *Come on Kati, give me a clue.*

"Too bad that's not a diary," Tamra said.

"How I wish."

"What else is in there other than appointment times?" she asked, dropping a pile of junk mail she had been sorting through into a trash basket.

Adam leafed the pages. "Random reminders like don't forget the hand powder, pick up athletic tape, bring along towels. There is one here I don't quite understand. It's entered on a Friday, exactly one week before the bridge incident. Apparently, she was intending to go bridge jumping on that day."

"What does it say?" Tamra asked, dividing her attention between a spreadsheet she had called up on her computer and his ruminations regarding the planner.

"If I'm deciphering her chicken scratches correctly, it says bridge jumping and below that clothing options, followed by tee-hee in parentheses. You're a woman. What could she mean by clothing options? Is she undecided as to what to wear for the day?"

Tamra took her eyes from the computer. "Let me see," she said.

Adam walked to her desk to show her the entry in question. She studied the note for a moment. "First of all, it's not clothing options, it's *clothing optional*. The tee-hee should tell you what she had in mind. Maybe Katie Carew was not the wholesome girl everyone has in mind," she pointed out, a smile emerging on her face.

Adam examined the entry once more. *Thank you, Kati.*

"Tamra, I want you to drop what you're doing. I have to leave for a parent-teachers conference at Noelle's school. While I'm gone, I'd like for you to find the number of a contact person for an organization called the Lacoochee Nature Club. It is based somewhere in Pasco County. I'm told it is the oldest nudist club in the state of Florida, so locating it should be a snap for you."

Tamra looked at her boss like it was the start of one of their occasional silly sessions. "You say that as if I have intimate knowledge of nudist clubs," she said, as he headed for the door.

"Well, do you?" he asked, with a hand on the door and a mischievous grin on his face.

"If you must know…yes," she said, returning the grin in kind.

Adam hesitated. "Care to explain?"

"On your return," she said. "Right now, you have a parent-teachers conference to attend. Remember?"

———

The parent-teachers conference was not unlike others he attended. Teachers talked, and he mostly listened. For parents of a straight-A student like Noelle, it was an academic love fest. With her thirst for knowledge, she personified the old adage that said the more you know, the more you come to realize how much you don't know, so keep at it. He would have liked to have patted himself on the back for her attitude but instead stuck to the belief his adoptive daughter's insatiable intellectual curiosity was a trait inherited from her deceased biological mother, a school teacher herself. Despite Noelle's academic excellence, Adam was enough of a worrier to find reason for concern in her grades, no matter their lofty status. Could they also be an indication she was an underachiever? Did school work come so easy to her that the straight A's reflected what she already knew rather than what she had learned? When he brought this to her teachers' attention, they all replied in one manner or the other that the question to be addressed by both the parent and teacher in this circumstance is whether the student is putting in the effort to achieve those grades. The answer from both the parent and teachers in Noelle's case was yes. Now and then Adam would have to do a little prodding, but that was to be expected, given the outside pressures on her time, like learning how to hit a rising softball crossing the outside corner of home plate.

Two hours later Adam was back in the office. "Any luck with the Lacoochee Nature Club contact?" he asked Tamra.

"Here you go," she said, ripping off a slip of paper from a desk note pad and handing it to him.

He looked at the name, number, and city scribbled on the paper.

"Jason Howard…Zepherhills," he said aloud before returning to his desk to dial the number.

Adam identified himself to the man with the spirited voice on the other end of the line, leaving out for the time being his profession. He started off by mentioning his surprise run-in along the river bank with a couple of members of the club.

"You don't recognize my voice?" Howard asked. "That was me and a fellow club member you ran into. Did you change your mind about joining? We're always looking for new members."

"No, my purpose in calling goes back to what you had to say about your club being the oldest nudist club in the state. Can you tell me exactly how old?"

"I can't tell you exactly. It's a little cloudy as to our actual start-up date. I've been told by others we date back to the thirties. Why do you ask?"

"I'm conducting some historical research having to do with the Withlacoochee River," Adam said, stretching the truth. "I suppose you could title my project 'Life Along the Withlacoochee,' since I'm trying to cover all aspects."

"Is this some kind of government project?"

"Yes, I'm doing this as part of a government local history project."

"How can we help?"

"What I'm looking for is someone in your group whose membership dates back to the early forties, someone who could provide me first-hand observations of life along the river in all its forms."

"Hmm…interesting," Jason said, settling into a thoughtful tone. "Presently, we have no active members who date back that far, which is probably not surprising, since we're talking about people nearly seventy to eighty years old."

"No, not surprising at all," Adam said, resignation creeping into his voice. "I appreciate your…"

"Wait a second," Jason said. "Now that I think about it, there is a former member in that age range who keeps in touch with some of the club's members."

"Her name?"

"Virginia Perkins…Ginny to her friends."

"Do you have her phone number by chance?"

"I'm looking at it right now. One of my responsibilities as Secretary of the Membership Committee is to keep current the club's directory, including information for past members that becomes available. However, it might be best if I gave her your number and let her decide whether she wants to be interviewed."

"Fair enough," Adam said and gave him his number.

"I'll call her now," Jason said.

Adam dropped the receiver into its cradle and turned his attention to Tamra. "Now back to your nudist camp episode. You were saying?"

She cast him a sidelong smile. "I've since decided to exercise my right to privacy and keep it private. This is one of those things best left to the imagination," she said and immediately changed the subject. "Tell me, do sheriffs' departments ever hire private investigators to work cases?"

Adam quieted his imagination long enough to answer the question. "Yes, they do, especially for undercover work. The law places restrictions on law enforcement personnel that a P. I. might not be bound by. There's also the cost saving factor. Temporary hires are not eligible for those generous government benefits. During periods of stiff budget cuts like the one we're currently experiencing, temporaries are an attractive option."

"Then why doesn't the department put you on its temporary payroll for this case? It seems only fair you be compensated."

Adam strolled over to Tamra's desk and took a seat on the edge of it. "We are being compensated. This is potentially a criminal case and at the moment the sheriff's department is running legal interference for us. As I see it, we've settled into a mutually beneficial working relationship."

"Which means you, and me, and they will end up either sinking or swimming together," his office manager pointedly responded.

"Hey, look on the bright—"

Tamra's desk phone abruptly rang. A moment later she had the receiver tucked under her chin. "A Ginny Perkins wishes to speak with you," she whispered.

He hustled back to his desk to take the call. "Adam Fraley here."

"Mr. Fraley, this is Ginny Perkins. I'm told you wish to speak with me," she said in a soft, clear voice, accented by age.

"Yes, Jason tells me you are the person I should talk to if I want to learn everything I can about life along the Withlacoochee River in the early 1940s."

"By 'life' you mean what?"

"Recreational activities, wildlife scene, bridge construction, traffic flow, floods, droughts, wartime impact on tourism…anything you know that might provide some insight into the culture at the time."

"Well, I certainly spent a good share of my time with the river," she said. "I may not be able to offer you an academic perspective, but I can provide you a laywoman's up close and personal one, if that would interest you."

"Good enough," Adam said eagerly. "Would you then be willing to meet with me for an in-person interview, say tomorrow morning, if it fits your schedule?"

"That would be fine. Where would you like to meet?"

"How about along the river where your former club gathers. I could meet you on the abandoned bridge, say at ten in the morning."

"I will see you then, Mr. Fraley."

"Why didn't you go ahead and conduct the interview over the phone," Tamra asked from across the room. "It would have saved you a lot of time and travel."

"What have I told you about telephone versus face-to-face interviews? With in-person you can build a rapport, establish a trust, not to mention all the non-verbal communication that is there to be had."

"Especially when you are sans clothes," she cracked.

"Careful, you're raising a topic best left to the imagination, remember?"

"I stand corrected," she said. "Anyway, have a good trip and don't forget to pack your birthday suit."

———

Ginny Perkins stood near one of the remaining railings of the broken Withlacoochee abandoned bridge, gazing out over the rippling surface of the meandering stream when Adam approached her. She was wearing a straw sun hat, white tunic, jeans, and hiking boots. In her hand she clutched what looked to be a large sketch folder. "I've always enjoyed the view from here. It's like watching the world move in slow motion," she said upon his arrival, foregoing for the moment any introduction.

Adam stood silent by her side, reluctant to break the spell the scene appeared to be having on her. Below them and beyond, the river wound its path through a myriad of thick vegetation bordering its banks. Lingering patches of river fog hung low over the stream, waiting to be dissipated by the sun's morning rays. Far away, a gathering of hawks performed lazy eights in the balmy air, while from the nearby water's edge a pair of great blue herons took to flight in tandem, their outstretched wings beating them slowly skyward.

"You're right. The world here sometimes seems close to stopping," he said, breaking the silence. "Let's hope the man upstairs doesn't apply the brakes to it anytime soon."

She turned to him. "Oh, I can stop it-with this," she said, patting her sketchbook.

"Ms. Perkins, Adam Fraley," he said, holding out his hand in belated greeting.

"Call me Ginny," she said, taking it. "Why don't we head down to the club's gathering place for our chit-chat? It will afford us some privacy, though everything around here is pretty much private."

Adam followed her off the bridge and through the same thickets of trees and brush bordering the river bank he had previously traversed. He was determined this time to avoid any cockle burrs lying in wait. On reaching the opening, both seated themselves on logs placed side by side inside the clearing.

"The club's idea of furniture," she said, patting the log.

"No upholstering required," he quipped.

She chuckled. "Club members always made sure they brought along two towels…one for sitting on and one for drying off."

"How long were you a club member?" Adam asked, carefully picking from his jeans the cockle burrs who eschewed his determination.

"I joined in 1939 and remained with them until 1980. You would be right in thinking I was on top of the seniority list."

"What was the atmosphere here like during the war years?"

"Much the same as any other year," she said. "We did have one fellow who was wounded early on in the conflict and ended up here after being released from duty and sent home to the States. He chose this spot to get as far away from the war as he could, including any news of it."

"I'm surprised he even mentioned it," Adam said, finishing the removal of cockle burrs. "Most vets don't want to discuss it."

"There is an expectation of privacy within the club. Many members offer only first names during introductions. Many also prefer not to divulge their occupations for professional reasons."

"Care to divulge yours, now that you are no longer an official member?" Adam asked with an easy smile.

"I was and am to this day the proverbial starving artist," she said, patting the sketchbook she clutched against her bosom.

She had the eyes of a thirty-year-old, Adam observed, riveted by the spell they cast. "What sort of art work?" he asked.

A family of ducks loudly quacked their presence on their swim upstream, momentarily halting the conversation.

"Sketching," she replied upon their passing. "Some call it doodling."

"I'm guessing it's several steps up from doodling," he said. "Your favorite subjects to sketch are?"

"The human form for number one. I also enjoy doing plants and animals."

"Were any of the human forms those of your former club mates?"

"No, none whatsoever," she said instantly. "I would never violate the privacy rules. That would have freaked them out as much as the binocular people did and still do."

"By binocular people you mean peeping toms?"

"No, bird watching groups. You could see them standing on the bridge or behind trees with their binoculars swinging back and forth like synchronized periscopes. We were never sure it was us or the birds they were scoping out."

"Snowbirds snooping on nature's own," Adam said.

"Oh, no," she quickly corrected him. "They and the tourists didn't start flocking down here until after the war. The binocular people were from these parts."

Adam looked past Ginny's shoulder. "I see there's an opening in the tree branches giving you an unobstructed view of the bridge."

"Yes, the opening has always been there, clear back to the early days of the club. You'd think the growth of vegetation over the years would have altered it, but it hasn't," she said, eyeing nature's window. "And, yes, we could easily see the bridge and the people occasionally wandering it. The nice part is they had a hard time seeing us, unless we were taking a swim or lounging on the bank, which I often did to sketch."

"I understand the inland swamps are the source of the river," he said.

"Yes, it originates in the swamps and is swelled along the way by the flow from springs."

Adam clasped his hands, rested his forearms on his thighs, and leaned in for his next question, telegraphing the seriousness of it. "I have a specific question for you, Ginny. It has to do with an incident that occurred on the bridge back in 1943, June 18 on a Friday morning to be exact."

A smile slowly formed on the elderly woman's weathered face.

"Why are you smiling?" Adam asked, somewhat taken aback by the reaction.

"When I called your office, the young lady answered, 'Adam Fraley Private Investigations.' It led me to believe this had more to do with a specific event rather than a series or decade of events."

"That obvious, huh?"

She nodded. "But go ahead with your question. I didn't mean to interrupt your line of thought."

Adam told the story of Roland Westwood and the Carew twins from the beginning to the present, leaving out no details. By the time he had finished, a beam of advancing sunlight, filtering through the trees, had reached where she was sitting, cloaking her in an ethereal light.

At first, she said nothing in response to the story, but then lowered the large sketch folder she had been clutching close to her bosom to her lap and opened it. She flipped through the pages until she landed on a chosen one. Taking the opened folder in both hands, she stepped over to where Adam was sitting and laid it face up on his lap. "Perhaps this will interest you," she said and returned to her log.

Adam gazed down at the opened folder in his lap, before leafing through several of its pages. It was his turn to at first say nothing, but then spoke. "Ginny, would you be willing to accompany me to the county prosecutor's office?"

"Of course, Adam."

CHAPTER ELEVEN

"The prosecutor's office called. The preliminary hearing is set for Thursday morning at nine," Adam's office manager announced upon his arrival at work.

"I was just in his office yesterday morning. He must have received word of the scheduling later in the day."

"Two days to prepare. I hope you have all your ducks in a row."

"We only have two of them...Westwood and Ginny Perkins," he said, settling into his desk chair.

"One of them may have been shot down already," Tamra said.

"How's that?" Adam asked, taken aback by the news.

"The D. A.'s office wanted me to pass along to you the message Westwood has a military desertion charge on his record."

"Oh, great...something of course he didn't bother to tell us. How do they propose to handle it? The defense is sure to bring it up. Credibility of a witnesses is key to any case."

"They said they will handle it when the time comes and left it at that. He also asked me to pass along word that Bob Ballard has agreed a polygraph test be given to Westwood."

"He is willing to roll the dice. That surprises me. I'm now

beginning to wonder if this was such a good idea. He must know something about Westwood we don't."

"The desertion charge for one thing," she said.

"We need to place a greater emphasis on screening clients, Tamra."

"This one is on me. It was my referral," she said. "I should have known better."

"Nah, it's not like I haven't taken on personal referrals before that have gone sour," he pointed out. "The lesson is we need to be careful with our screening. It's particularly important in cases that are potentially criminal. The goal is to make sure a case is a good fit for us." What he wanted to add but didn't was that Roland Westwood's plight was no longer uppermost in his mind. Fair or not, Kati Carew had become his subject of interest.

"Background checking of clients takes time, Adam, people time. It's not an easy thing to do, if you want it done right."

"I hear what you're saying. It also raises the touchy matter of investigating your own clients. They don't sign on for that."

"As a first step, why don't I revise the intake form, make it abundantly clear as to what we will and will not accept, and what screening is required," she suggested.

"Good idea. Then we can work on the interview process. What is it they say? The resume gets you the interview, the interview gets you the job, or in our case, a private eye on your side. How's that for a future campaign ad—a private eye on your side?"

Tamra rolled her eyes and returned to the matter at hand. "Here's hoping nothing turns up on Ginny Perkins that could sink the case," she said.

"She's not our client. She's officially been placed in the hands of the prosecutor."

Adam stood and stretched his arms. "Anything else of importance on the agenda today?"

"You asked me to track down Timmy Whalen. Well, I checked with former employers of his in Florida, Central America, and Southeast Asia with no luck. One of them did give me an address and phone number for his family in New Zealand, so I ended up calling them directly. His father answered the phone and was very friendly." Tamra paused to sigh a breath. "I'm sorry to tell you this, Adam, but it turns out your friend Timmy was killed in an accident several years ago on some remote Pacific Island I have never heard of."

A sudden pall settled over Adam. "Did he give any details?"

"Yes. He said Timmy was picking coconuts from a tree adjacent to the edge of a cliff and fell while reaching for one. He landed on the rocks at the bottom." Tamra looked up from the notes she was reading from. "Why the smile, Adam?"

The account had lifted the pall from Adam as quickly as it had settled over him "You would have had to have known Timmy to understand the reason for the smile," he said. "He was always reaching too far, in the groves and in life."

Tamra continued. "His father did ask who was inquiring about his son and I gave him your name. He recalled Timmy talking about you in his letters from Florida and the fun times you two had together. I took the liberty of expressing your belated condolences, Adam, and he in response wanted me to pass along his thanks for the friendship you extended to his son."

Adam nodded his appreciation. "Anything else on the agenda?"

"Yes, your daughter," she answered

Adam dropped back down into his chair. "Not another suspension, I hope."

"The opposite, as a matter of fact. In case you're not aware, her first playoff game is days away and she is unprepared to compete, if you don't mind me saying."

"Unprepared in what way?"

"To hit a rising softball, the most difficult pitch in the game. The team they're playing, the North Bay Sharks, has a pitcher by the name of Rita Brownback. They call her the 'Backbreaker' for the way she is able to cause hitters to go through all sorts of contortions in their efforts to hit the pitch. There have been exhibition matches pitting top major league hitters against top softball pitchers and the hitters usually come out on the short end, unable to hit a fast-rising softball. Why don't major league pitchers utilize the underhand motion, you may ask? Well, there have been pitchers who've had an underhand delivery, but the effect is not the same. The shorter distance between the mound and home plate in softball has a lot to do with it. A softball hitter just doesn't have the time to react to the pitch. Brownback has perfected it to the level of terrorizing opposing batters. The bad news is she's scheduled to be on the mound for the game."

"You make it sound like an impossible task," Adam said.

"Not impossible, if you're fully prepared for what's to come."

"Isn't that the coach's job?"

"The coach is about as competent at coaching as Harlan Weeks is at calling balls and strikes," she said. "He belongs in the recreational leagues. You know, the ones playing for the amusement of the beer-in-the-hand fans."

"Slow-pitch ball, my kind of game," Adam observed. "You hit the ball as far as you can, run as hard as you can, and for as far as you can."

"As opposed to the game your daughter is playing where you get a runner on base and move her around with a bunt, walk, stolen base, hit batter, error, passed ball, or slap hit."

Adam slid his chair back, folded his arms across his chest, and propped his feet up on the desk, drawing an instant frown from his office manager. He quickly lowered them. "Tell me, when did you become a student of the game?" he asked.

"The answer is in your question. When I was a student in school, my father talked me into going out for the team. I also played in a summer league."

"Position?"

"Pitcher."

"Well now, that explains everything."

"It does?"

"Yes, your interest and knowledge of the game, your competitiveness, your regard for Noelle's success…"

"You think I'm re-living my childhood dreams through her, like parents are wont to do?"

The conversation was veering fast in a direction he cared not to go. Parenting was off the table, as far as he was concerned, and he intended to keep it off. It was one step away from motherhood, a topic best left for another time and place. "No, I believe you have the best interests of Noelle at heart, Tamra. So, what do you propose for her game preparation?" he asked, steering the conversation back onto the playing field.

"I propose you and I take her to Parker Field this evening to work on her swing."

"What time?" he asked, not about to dampen her enthusiasm.

"Seven o'clock. That should give us an hour of daylight."

"Is the field available?"

"I've already checked with the parks department. There are no organized activities scheduled for this evening. Barring a pick-up game, we should have the field to ourselves."

"And what is my role?" he asked.

Tamra flashed him a satisfying smile. "To shag balls."

———

Parker Field was a throwback to the old neighborhood ballparks of the past. A step up from sandlot status, it was squeezed between houses and streets in the middle-class section of town. The field itself was mostly solid rock covered with a few inches of dirt and random patches of grass. A wooden fence, wall-papered with worn advertisements, surrounded the perimeter of the outfield. Running diagonally from behind the third-base foul line to the first base line was a wooden grandstand, separated from the playing field by wire fencing. Wooden benches, backed against a restraining wall, served as dugouts. Altogether, a fitting setting and relaxing atmosphere for not only pickup games but the playoff contest less than a week away, Adam decided.

Evening shadows stretched to the far reaches of the outfield by the time Tamra took to the mound to put Noelle through her hitting exercises. The stands were empty, except for three uniformed teenage boys who apparently had hung around from an earlier team practice to shoot the breeze or perhaps enjoy the sight of Tamra striding around the mound in the pair of short blue shorts and halter top she had decided to wear. Oblivious to the attention, she commenced delivering pitch after pitch from a rapid windmill windup in an effort to mimic the intimidating style of Rita Brownback. From where he stood on the edge of the outfield, directly behind second base, Adam gained an appreciation of the difficulty of hitting the "rise ball" as it was called. The pitch required of the hitter a totally unnatural way of hitting a ball. Furthermore, Tamra was hurling it with great velocity, though from the way she described it, nowhere near the velocity with which Brownback unleashed it.

"Keep your eye on the ball and your swing level," Tamra instructed in a raised voice from the mound. "All you want to do is put the bat on the ball. Don't slap at it, meet it."

Putting the bat on the ball was no easy task for Noelle as she swung futilely at the oncoming pitches, managing to foul off a couple or top a grounder back to the mound.

"Noelle, move your stance closer to the front of the batter's box," Tamra called to her. "See if you can meet the pitch before it approaches its apex."

The results were no better as Noelle continued to flail at the plate. With each swing and miss, she would stamp her feet in frustration, a signal to Adam it was time for a break. He knew whatever task was assigned his daughter, whether in the classroom or on the playing field, she would tackle it relentlessly, almost to a fault, leaving no room for failure. There was no reason to become obsessed with hitting a pitch, no matter the challenge it presented. It was, after all, only a game they were playing, he reasoned, realizing at once he was sounding much like Karen Cox from the league office.

"Time out!" Adam shouted, whereupon he jogged from his short center-field position, past second base and the mound to home plate to confer with his daughter. "You take my spot in the outfield and shag balls. I'll show you how to hit the rise ball," he said, loud enough to reach Tamra's ears.

Whereas Noelle's competitive spirit was always on display, Tamra's was always lurking beneath the surface, so what better way to institute a break in the proceedings than to bring it to the fore, he thought.

She stood on the mound, a devilish smile forming on her face. "Are you sure you're ready for this?" she asked.

Adam took a couple of practice swings. "Bring it on," he said forcefully, fully aware of what was about to be delivered.

Tamra wound her arm and cut loose a fastball with such force it nearly toppled her from the mound.

If he hadn't expected it, he might not have been able to twist his body in time to avoid the full brunt of it. As it was, the pitch struck him in the butt, the preferred spot for the batter, given all the choices of where to be hit. He froze for an instant, his back to the mound. He heard a loud giggle in the distance, coming from his daughter. Suddenly, he spun around, flipped the bat off to the side, and rushed the mound in feigned fury.

"Adam!" Tamra yelped in reaction, as he grabbed her around the waist, lifted her over his shoulder, and carted her to the outfield, depositing her back on her feet next to where Noelle stood. "You go back to hitting," he said to his daughter. "I'll do the pitching and Tamra will do the shagging."

"Your father does not know how to take a brush-back pitch," Tamra emphatically said.

"I beg your pardon. I took it right where you're supposed to take it," he said, patting his posterior.

Taking his turn on the mound, Adam proceeded to lob soft balls to Noelle who sprayed them around the field, keeping Tamra busy. A few minutes of the toned-down workout was all it took for Tamra to break her silence.

"Adam, this is doing her no good," she called from the outfield.

"Daddy, she's right," his daughter chimed in. "I need to prepare for the rise ball, not a lob ball. Anybody can hit those."

Adam acquiesced, motioning with a wave of the arm, as if to a bullpen, for Tamra to take the mound. He, in turn, returned to the edge of the outfield to while away the time, hoping she could at least slap one of Tamra's deliveries his way. Alas, it was not to be despite his office manager peppering her with advice.

"Don't grip the bat too hard, swing level or slightly upward. Stride into the pitch. Be patient," she urged from the mound between deliveries. Noelle did manage to make better contact with the ball, but nowhere near the level required to drive solid hits to the outfield.

So it went, pitch after pitch, swing after swing, dribbler after dribbler, until darkness ended the session, emptying Parker Field of players and onlookers alike. Up next, the playoff game that would end or prolong the season, but first, there was a courtroom encounter looming on the horizon.

CHAPTER TWELVE

FROM WHERE HE SAT IN THE SPECTATORS' SECTION, ADAM'S immediate overall impression of the courtroom was one of polished and burnished brass, made radiant by beams of morning sunlight angling down on the furnishings through tall bay windows located on each side of the stone building. Occupying the elevated judge's bench was an elderly robed man who sat with a slight stoop to his shoulders. Stringy, straw hair ran randomly to the rim of his taut face, a few reaching to his hazel eyes. A pair of bifocals hung halfway down his aquiline nose, over which he peered at the assembled. Below him stood the court reporter's station, flanked by the plaintiff and defense tables. A witness box was positioned adjacent to the judge's bench. Perched further off to the side of the room was the jury box, empty for the purpose of the hearing. Stevens alone manned the plaintiff's table. Bob Ballard and his wife, whom he represented, occupied the defense table.

With her silky, swept-back ashen hair, well-preserved face, and overall distinguished look, Staci Ballard bore a strong resemblance to her husband. It was as if they were the twins whose story was about to be told. Both wore tailored gray suits in keeping with their handsome couple image.

Prior to the hearing, Stevens alerted the prosecution team to an issue concerning the judge, Harrison Steele. As he explained it, Steele at one time appointed Staci Carew, a mental health professional, as a neutral expert for the court in a proceeding involving a divorce custody issue over which he was presiding. The fact Steele was in no way related to Staci and had a good reputation among legal circles mitigated the circumstance in the eyes of Stevens. Steele was undoubtedly aware of the past connection but felt it was not a deal breaker or he would have removed himself from the case. A court-appointed expert witness is not based on a personal relationship but the credentials of the individual, Stevens noted. It was a routine procedure. Staci, in fact, had served as a courtroom expert in other trials presided over by other judges. It was not worth filing a motion to try and disqualify the judge, Stevens believed.

"For now, we'll let it pass," he said. The prosecutor had also informed Adam that he planned on calling only two witnesses to the stand, Westwood and Ginny Perkins. There was the possibility Adam would be called should Stevens deem it necessary. Otherwise, the testimony of Westwood and Perkins would be the determining factor in whether the case advanced beyond the preliminary stage, Stevens advised.

The judge banged his gavel, cleared his throat, and in a voice as gritty as his face called on the prosecutor to present his case.

Stevens gave an opening statement, essentially outlining the charges. When finished, the judge directed him to call his first witness to the stand.

Westwood was up first. Stevens walked him through his effort to reconnect with his first love, emphasizing the witness's original intent to meet with her once more before life ran out on him.

Adam kept his eyes on Staci who sat expressionless, her own eyes fixed on the witness as if he was a complete stranger. Not the kind of reunion his client had in mind, Adam mused. To say there was an unspoken tension between the two main players in the courtroom went without saying. It was stamped on Staci and Westwood's faces, despite their efforts to disguise it.

Stevens quickly moved to the matter of the bridge incident and the official sheriff's report, a copy of which he held in his hand. "You hired a private investigator to locate Staci Carew, is that correct?"

"Yes."

"And during the course of the investigation, the matter of the bridge incident surfaced. Correct?"

"Yes, the private investigator brought it to my attention."

"Bringing it to his attention was something you initially failed to do, right?"

"Right."

"Was it in the back of your mind that the incident might surface?"

"Yes, I thought it might."

"Were you happy or sad it did?"

"Both."

"Happy in what way?"

"Happy for the opportunity to bring the report to light again."

"In order to correct it?"

"Yes, if at all possible."

"Why wait all this time and why were you not forthcoming to begin with? Why all the subterfuge?"

"Fear. I did not want to be seen as an accomplice to a crime."

"We've all had the chance to read the report," Stevens said, waving the copy in his hand. "What in it needs to be corrected?"

"Most of it is correct."

"Except for?"

"Except for the fact Kati was not alone on the bridge."

"Who was there with her?"

"Her sister Staci and I were both there."

"How did that come to be?" Stevens asked, breaking into a back and forth stroll.

"Kati issued an invitation to us to join her at the bridge. She issued it through me. I was to invite her sister along."

"For what purpose? Bridge jumping?"

"No. Kati's intention was to practice her gymnastics routine in a highly pressurized atmosphere to help her prepare for upcoming competitions. She thought doing it on a bridge railing was one way of learning to perform under pressure."

"Was there another intention?"

"Yes, the primary one. It sprung from my idea to play peacemaker. I was concerned with the growing animosity between the two. It was obviously rising above the level of normal sibling rivalry. I thought a relaxed outing with just the three of us might open the lines of communication and ease the tensions. It was why I originally posed the idea to Kati for a bridge outing which later led to her invitation. She said her boyfriend would be out of town that particular day and her schedule was open. She was all in favor of it."

"The idea of a get-together was really yours."

"Yes."

A variance from his original story, Adam ruminated, but not a game changer. Ballard certainly was not going to pursue it and risk falling into the trap of acknowledging there was an invitation in the first place. No, he would continue to deny anything suggesting or claiming his wife was at the scene of an alleged crime.

"Did Staci agree to it?" Stevens asked.

"That was my mistake. I intentionally did not tell her for fear she would not agree to come. I should have known better, especially since it was Staci's old boyfriend who had taken up with Kati, after having parted ways with her sister."

Adam glanced at Staci to gauge a reaction but there was no change to the rigid facial expression she held fast to.

"Events didn't go as planned once Staci arrived on the scene?"

Westwood nodded his agreement. "The old antagonisms erupted immediately. I'm not sure if it was the boyfriend issue or not, but the transformation in Staci's temperament became evident the moment the two came within earshot of each other."

"Were words exchanged?"

"Not long after, yes, though nearly all of them were coming from Staci."

"What was Kati's reaction?"

"She tried to block out the barbs first by ignoring them and when that didn't work, she launched into her gymnastics routine."

"Right then and there?"

"Yes. She all at once shed her outer clothing, aligned herself alongside the railing, and mounted it in a single leap. She began to perform a routine that included handstands, backflips and several other movements. I found it both remarkable and risky that she could do this on a bridge rail with such ease. From what I had heard and read, she had world class potential, but not until that morning did I fully realize the extent of her talent."

Stevens glanced at the sheriff's report and shook his head, letting everyone know nothing of what they were hearing was on there. "You and Staci were positioned approximate to Kati while she was performing. Correct?"

"Yes, no more than a few feet away. Staci was behind her. I was in front of her."

"As she was performing, did her sister continue with the caustic comments?"

"Yes. Some were said to me but intended for her sister."

"Like?"

"'She sure likes to strut her stuff.'"

"Was there any specific comment aimed directly at her sister that you found particularly spiteful?"

"The instant Kati completed her routine and had her arms raised high in triumph, I asked her if it was an Olympic medal she was aiming for and she responded, 'That's my hope, Roland,' at which point Staci said, 'You aim to win at everything, don't you, Kati,' obviously referring to the boyfriend issue. 'I mean no harm to anyone,' Kati said, to which her sister snapped 'Bull-crap,' at which point she stepped forward and gave Kati a shove as she still stood on the railing."

Stevens paused a moment to let the vision sink in. "Not a nudge, not a bump, not a poke, but a shove," he said, thrusting his arms out to make the point. "Right?"

"Right."

"From behind her, right?"

"Right, she never saw it coming or else she might have been able to take some evasive action, as sure of foot as she was."

"The shove knocked her from the bridge?"

"Yes. She let out a yelp, dropped down hard on the railing, and tumbled off the bridge, striking her head on an abutment on the way down."

"What made you think that?" Stevens asked. "Did you see her hit her head?"

"I didn't need to see it. I heard it. There was a sickening thud as she fell. I knew it had to be her head for it to make that sound."

"What occurred immediately following the fall?"

"We both rushed to look over the railing. That's when we saw her body floating down the river."

"Face down?"

"Yes."

"Dead, you presumed?"

"From all outward appearances, dead or at least knocked unconscious."

"Then what?"

Westwood described the aftermath as he had related it to Adam in his office, ending with how she'd spoken in such a calm voice that he began to feel she—not he—was the reasonable one. After all, it was her sister they were talking about. How he'd come to believe her view should take priority. How she almost commanded him to leave and how he followed, as though at that point he was looking for any excuse to leave.

As the case unfolded in front of him, Adam was puzzled by Bob Ballard's passive reaction to the testimony. On several occasions he expected the defense attorney to jump in with objections to what could be interpreted as leading or opinion-loaded questions. Then it hit him again, the reason for his passivity. By inserting his objections into the testimony, he would be indirectly giving credence to the charge Staci and Westwood were present at the event. Ballard's strategy was a simple one, Adam concluded. Stick to arguing for the validity of the original report.

"So, it was you who first turned to exit the bridge in order to get to Kati," Stevens reaffirmed.

"Yes."

"And Staci did not follow your lead. Instead she began to argue otherwise."

"Correct."

"And reluctantly you ended up acceding to her demands."

"Correct."

"For what reason?"

"I was fearful of being charged as an accomplice; fearful of placing my future in jeopardy."

Stevens turned and strode slowly to the prosecutor's table before pivoting again to face the witness. "Mr. Westwood, what would you say is your lasting memory of the incident?"

Westwood looked to the ceiling as if hoping the answer might be scribbled there. "I'm not sure," he said, returning his attention to Stevens. "If anything, it was the look of shock on Kati's face the moment she realized what her sister had done to her."

"That's all your honor," the prosecutor said before taking a seat.

"Counsel, cross?" the judge asked Ballard.

"Yes, your honor."

Ballard took the floor wearing his passion on his sleeve. Defiance was shooting from his eyes. He was, after all, not only a defense attorney but a husband defending his wife and, more importantly, the family reputation to which he was tethered. He carried with him a copy of the incident report.

"You hired a private investigator. Correct?" he asked Westwood, knowing the answer.

"Yes."

"Hired him for what purpose?"

"To locate Staci. She was my first flame," he calmly stated to Staci's husband. "I always wondered what became of her."

Adam winced at the reference to his "first flame."

"You needed a P. I. for that when a few phone calls placed to the right people might have sufficed?"

"It was an option," Westwood answered, downplaying his choice.

"How did the matter of the bridge incident enter into the search sequence?"

"It entered into the discussion during the course of the P. I.'s investigation."

"The P. I. was the one to raise the matter?"

"Yes, he brought it to my attention."

"Surely, you had some inkling the bridge incident might come up."

"Yes, I knew there was a chance it would."

"Yet, it was not your primary intent in hiring the P. I.?"

"Not exactly."

Ballard threw his hands out in feigned frustration. "Oh, not exactly. This is getting a little confusing. Please explain."

"It was not my initial intent. I did wish to see Staci again but knew in the back of my mind there was the possibility the private investigator would unearth the incident. It is hard to separate the two."

"The incident as written in this report," Ballard said, raising high the copy he carried in hand. "The one you now say is false."

"Yes, for the most part."

"And once the incident was put into play by the P. I., you took the occasion to set the record straight, taking your revisionism to the sheriff and district attorney."

"Yes,"

"Convoluted way to set the record straight, don't you think?" Ballard asked, prowling the floor back and forth like a caged lion.

"Objection, you honor. Counsel is leading the witness," Stevens snapped.

"Sustained."

"You now say you lied in the official report."

"Yes, I did," Westwood stated forthrightly.

"Why?"

Westwood shifted in the witness chair, crossing one leg over the other. "Like I said, I was talked into it by Staci."

Adam was sure Stevens advised Westwood beforehand to say, 'Staci' and not 'your wife' when referencing Kati's sister. Otherwise, things would really get testy between the two, as though they weren't already.

"A college guy was talked into telling authorities a whopper of a lie by a high school girl. Is that it?"

"Yes."

"Do you have issues with dementia, Mr. Westwood?"

"Objection, your honor. Pure speculation," Stevens snapped.

"Sustained."

A good reason for the case not to go to a full trial, Adam reckoned. By then Ballard will have had a court order in hand to release Westwood's medical records.

"Did you have a romantic interest in Kati?"

"None whatsoever."

Good thing he wasn't hooked up to a polygraph machine when he answered that question, Adam mused, perhaps unfairly.

"How long after the bridge incident did your relationship with Staci end?"

Westwood pondered a moment. "A couple of months or so."

"Did you or Staci end the relationship?"

"Staci did."

"To your dissatisfaction?"

Westwood hunched his shoulders. "To my disappointment would be more accurate."

"Did you attempt to contact Staci following your breakup?"

"On occasion."

"Often enough for it to be considered stalking?"

"Objection, your honor. Leading the witness."

"Sustained."

"Did you receive a warning from Staci's father concerning your repeated attempts to contact her?"

Westwood hesitated. "It was more a request than a warning. As soon as he asked me to discontinue my efforts, I did. I decided then it was time to take a new direction in my life, so I packed up and joined the military."

Ballard stepped over to the defense table to pick up a sheet of paper and peruse it before resuming his questioning. "Regarding your stint in the military, were you at one time charged with going AWOL from your post?"

"Objection, your honor," Stevens called out. "Irrelevant to the case."

"Your honor," Ballard fired back. "The witness made it relevant by introducing the topic in his answer."

The judge removed his glasses and rubbed his eyes. "Overruled," he said and placed them back on. "The witness will answer the question."

"Yes, I was charged with being AWOL. My grandmother, who raised me, was in very ill health and I overstayed my allotted leave time to be with her a while longer."

"You in effect deserted your post." Ballard interjected.

"Objection, your honor. Defense counsel is not giving the witness the opportunity to answer the question."

"Objection sustained. Let the witness answer the question," the judge responded.

"I was never charged with desertion," Westwood explained. "Desertion is the intention to remain away permanently. The base commander ordered that I receive an Article 15, which is a non-judicial punishment. He also fined me and ordered me restricted to the base. Under those conditions, I was allowed to return to duty."

Ballard strolled to the defense table to deposit the sheet of notes he was carrying. He then turned to face Westwood. "I ask you, why should we believe you are telling us the truth now when you admittedly lied back then?"

"For one simple, but very important reason to me. I want to set the record straight before I leave this earth. I owe that to Kati."

"On the subject of lying, did law enforcement officials administer a polygraph test to you?"

"They did."

Adam knew it was coming. Stevens had advised the prosecution team prior to the hearing that the polygraph results had come in and were deemed inconclusive. Supposedly, this meant there was no determination whether Westwood was lying or not. However, since the prosecution's case was built almost solely on the notion Westwood was telling the truth, it was in effect a big plus for the defense.

"What were the results of the test?" Ballard asked, knowing full well what they were.

"They were inconclusive," Westwood said, a note of resignation in his reply.

"You expect the court to ignore a result that is not supportive of your testimony. Is that correct?"

Westwood paused, as if to fashion an answer. "I expect the court to consider all the evidence," he replied.

Nice piece of damage control, Adam thought.

"By stating the original report is inaccurate, there is no intent on your part to exact a measure of revenge on Staci for dumping you?"

"Absolutely not. I like Staci. I continue to have fond thoughts of her."

Ouch, Adam thought. That had to sting a bit, though it could have been worse if he had said dreams instead of thoughts.

"You don't consider your pursuit of the case a twisted way of expressing fondness for the defendant?" Ballard asked, his question soaked with sarcasm.

"Objection, your honor."

"Sustained."

"That's all, your honor," Ballard said, a look of satisfaction on his face.

"Hanging by a thread," was Adam's first reaction to the testimony. Westwood's cross examination could not have gone much better from the defense counsel's standpoint. Ballard had delivered some body blows, enough to cast serious doubt on whether the case would advance beyond the preliminary round.

"Redirect, counselor?" the judge asked Stevens.

"Yes, your honor," he responded, rising to approach the witness stand.

"Mr. Westwood, you were aware there was a tension in the air between Staci and Kati. You said your purpose in proposing the get-together to Kati was to patch things up between the two. Can you tell the court if you did anything specific to facilitate the lessening of tension?"

Westwood nodded. "As a matter of fact, I did. Right after we arrived and were approaching the bridge, Staci realized she had mistakenly left her sunscreen in the car and went back to fetch it. While she was away, I broached the subject with Kati, telling her I was concerned with the state of their relationship and that I would hate to see it deteriorate further for I liked both of them. I reminded her this was a good opportunity for the two of them to begin the healing."

"Her response to your concern?"

"She said not to worry. There was nothing between them that could destroy her love for her sister."

Courtroom eyes, including Adam's, turned to Staci. For the first time in the trial, she lowered her eyes from the witness stand to the desk in front of her, a reaction that also caught the attention of the prosecutor, Adam noted.

"Thank you, Mr. Westwood. That will be all," Stevens said.

"Next witness?" the judge asked.

Stevens shifted his lanky frame to address the judge. "I'd like to call Ms. Ginny Perkins to the stand, your honor."

She had tied her hair back into a bun and jettisoned her jeans in favor of a long floral-patterned skirt reaching to her sandals. She proceeded to walk to the witness stand with a delicate step, acknowledging the presence of the judge with a slight bow. To Adam she appeared very much a light spirit amid the heavy surroundings.

"You're an artist, Ms. Perkins?" Stevens began.

"Yes," she said in her soft, cultured voice.

"What kind of art?"

"Penciled sketches, generally speaking, primarily of the human form, though I also sketch animals, especially pets, as well as natural landscapes."

"You were a longtime member of the Lacoochee Nature Club, a nudist club, correct?"

"Yes, I was an active member at one time."

"For how long were you a member?"

"I was a member for thirty-five years."

"Can you tell the court what years?"

"From 1940 to 1975."

"When and where did the club meet?"

"We met every Friday morning along the banks of the Withlacoochee River."

"A short distance from the abandoned Withlacoochee bridge?"

"Yes, about fifty yards or so."

"You would have met the Friday morning of June 18, 1943. Correct?"

"There were very few times we ever canceled a meeting. I recall a couple of occasions during hurricane seasons when we ended up canceling sessions, but I don't believe we ever canceled one as early as June. So, the answer to your question is yes, we would have met on that morning."

"Do you specifically recall being there for the meeting in question?"

"Yes."

"Can you tell the court if you witnessed any activity on the abandoned bridge on that particular morning?"

"Yes, I did. I often would set aside time to sketch during the course of our gatherings. To ensure the group's privacy, we met in a clearing that was surrounded by thick foliage. However, from where I sat and sketched, there was an opening in the vegetation sufficient enough to allow me a clear view of the bridge."

"What did you see?"

"Young people engaging in a favorite pastime of theirs, bridge jumping."

"How many young people?"

"Three, two girls and a boy."

"They were there together?"

"They were interacting with each other. One of the girls and the boy were dressed in street clothes. The other girl was dressed in a leotard. I would not have paid much attention to them, if the girl in the leotard at one point had not hopped up on the bridge rail. I thought she was intending to dive into the river. Instead, she launched into a series of gymnastic moves while atop the railing. I remembered thinking those are not the moves of an untrained gymnast."

"What happened then?"

"When she completed her routine, she stood for a few seconds in a kind of triumphant pose with her arms held high. I turned away for a moment to continue my sketching when I heard a yelp coming from the bridge. I quickly looked up to see the girl gymnast tumbling toward the water. I assumed the bridge jumping had begun. I next saw the jumper's two companions leave the bridge. I assumed to rejoin her along the banks somewhere."

"You were upstream from the bridge?"

"Yes."

"Did you consider anything you witnessed out of the ordinary?"

"Other than the performance of the one girl on the bridge railing, I considered it normal, a few kids out for a fun time."

"Over the following days, you saw nothing in the papers or heard anything on the radio regarding a fatal accident on the bridge?"

"No, I seldom listened to the radio or read the papers. This was during the war years of course and that dominated the news. I tuned it out. Plus, I lived a good distance from the bridge, outside the range of the local media outlets. Communications back in those days were not what they are today. It was easy to escape the headlines and air waves whether you wished to or not."

"Once the three individuals were out of sight, you returned to your pencil sketching, correct?"

"Correct."

Stevens walked to an area adjacent to the witness box where a large easel had been positioned atop a temporary stand. He was about to stage some courtroom theater.

"If I may, your honor, I would like to show the court the series of sketches Ms. Perkins completed on the day of the incident. These are enlarged photocopies of the originals, which have been entered into the record."

Stevens flipped back a blank cover sheet to expose to the courtroom audience the first of the sketches. The impact on those in attendance was palpable and for good reason, for there staring them in the face was a life-sized rendering of Kati Carew standing tall on the bridge railing in her closing triumphant stance.

No doubt about it, Adam thought. Ginny Perkins had put a face and figure for what up until now for most was a vague vision from the past.

Stevens next flipped through six more sketches showing a complete sequence of Kati's routine. If he had flipped through them in rapid succession, he would have recreated a 1940s animated movie, Adam mused.

"I'd like to point out to the court the witness dated the sketches," the prosecutor said, pointing to the "June 18, 1943" entered at the bottom of the one on display.

The rendering of Kati hovered over the courtroom like a celestial apparition. "Beauty is proportional," Adam recalled Ginny saying when he first laid eyes on the drawings. "Ideal lines, particularly those represented by human forms in motion, are ideally proportionate and beautiful to behold. It was a moment in time I felt compelled to capture," she'd said.

"These drawings represent what you saw on the day in question. Is that correct?" Stevens asked.

"Yes," she responded. "I draw from short term memory. I take a good look at the subject and then look away to sketch it."

"To reiterate, there were two other individuals on the bridge with Kati?"

"Yes, that is correct."

"You did not sketch them, right?"

"Correct. I was only interested in the girl atop the railing."

Stevens moved from the easel to the plaintiff's table to check his notes.

"Mr. Stevens, may I offer an opinion regarding this trial?" Ginny suddenly asked, startling nearly everyone in the courtroom.

"Objection, your honor!" Ballard bellowed, the request catapulting the defense attorney from his chair.

From the look on his face, the prosecutor appeared to Adam as though he might have no objection to the objection, wary as attorneys are of a witness veering off script and this certainly was not in anybody's script.

"Overruled counsel," the judge responded. "The witness is entitled to a lay opinion as long as it's rationally based and relevant to the case. Proceed Ms. Perkins."

"Well, as I mentioned before, I tuned out most of the war news, not because I didn't believe in the cause or lacked interest in its progress. No, it was for a much more personal reason. One of my two sisters was killed in the war. She was an Army nurse, a year younger than I. As siblings, we had our share of rivalries and jealousies, some more severe than others, including physical altercations, the pushing and shoving kind. The only difference between ours and the Carew girls was that none of our pushing and shoving took place on a bridge railing. Otherwise, our fits of pique might have had a similar tragic ending. Despite the efforts of our parents to defuse them, the altercations reached an intensity that led to my sister joining the Army for the sole reason to get away from me. This was toward the beginning of the war. Shortly thereafter, we received word of her death in the crash of a military transport plane."

Ginny paused to ponder her sketch of Kati Carew, holding her gaze to it as she continued with her account. "I have a sketch of my sister similar to this one in its style, one I drew a day following word of her death, one to help me cope with the loss from that day forward." She paused again before pressing on. "What did I learn from losing a sister at such a young age and in that manner? For one thing, the guilt is forever. For another, there is no sentence that could surpass the one I've already served."

Ginny turned her attention back to the judge. "Thank you for allowing me my say, your honor."

In keeping with the celestial tone injected into the proceedings by the Kati sketch, Adam noted another higher phenomenon taking place in the courtroom. The set-in-stone eyes of Staci Ballard were leaking tears like some miraculous religious icon. The loss of her composure, silent though it was, commanded the attention of those in attendance, none more so than her husband who appeared in panic mode. The defense attorney was standing and glancing nervously around the room, as if seeking help or perhaps an exit through which he could flee the scene.

"This thing is not going into extra innings," Adam whispered to himself.

The judge tapped his gavel. "Let's take a break," he said. "I'd like to see the prosecutor, defense counsel, and defendant in my chamber, please," he added, before rising to leave.

Except for a few court personnel and a sprinkling of spectators, the room emptied, leaving Adam time to speculate on the turn of events. Instead, he focused on another issue occupying his mind that required a decision. Often his indecisiveness on one matter was alleviated by his concentration on another. In this instance, the trial and its pending outcome soaked up all his reluctance to address a secondary issue that had been weighing on his mind for some time. Now was the moment, he'd decided, to end the procrastination.

Hustling from the courtroom, he headed for the courthouse lobby and an indoor phone booth. Quickly, lest he begin debating the propriety of his intention and change his mind, he deposited a quarter and dialed his office.

"Adam Fraley Private Investigations," came the sultry toned voice.

"How are things on the home front?"

"Quiet and on your end, any decision?"

"We're on a break," he said, before braving the purpose of his call. "I have a question for you."

"Okay."

"Do you have anything planned for this evening?"

"No…why? Has something come up?"

"Would you like to go out to dinner?"

"With you?" she asked, packing as much shock as a person could into two words.

"Yes…with me."

She paused for what seemed like the time it took to plan the Normandy invasion. "You mean like a dinner date?"

"Yes, a date for dinner."

Another pause that did nothing for his confidence. "Don't be afraid to say no," he added, anticipating the answer.

"Oh, I'm not afraid to say no,"

"I being your boss and all…"

"The answer is yes, Adam," she said, mercifully putting an end to his awkwardness.

"I'll pick you up at your place about seven."

"That will be fine. I'll see you then."

He hung up thinking, *I've just asked my office manager out!*

If not for the distraction of the trial, he might never have been able to summon up the courage to ask for the date, what with all the potentially disastrous consequences. As it was, he had one favorable verdict in his pocket and could now head back to the courtroom for the attempt at a second.

———

The break was taking longer than expected when the bailiff came in to inform Adam that the prosecution team was gathering in a second-floor meeting room. Something was in the works, he reckoned.

He was the last to arrive, joining Westwood and Ginny Perkins at a conference table headed by the prosecutor. A yellow scratch pad filled with notes lay open before him. One glance around the table at faces filled with anticipation and Stevens was ready to deliver the news. "It's over," he said with finality. "We've reached a plea deal.

Essentially, it is this—the defense agrees to plead *nolo contender,* no contest—to a charge of involuntary manslaughter in exchange for a suspended sentence. As a result of the plea, the original incident report will be corrected."

Stevens glanced down at his notes. "Here are the central considerations that led to the deal. One, the state of Florida has no statute of limitations for a felony resulting in a death. Two, from the defense's perspective, there was a good chance the case was headed to a full trial. Third, and this is the mitigating circumstance that spurred the plea deal—Staci Ballard, it was revealed, has recently been diagnosed as having terminal pancreatic cancer, a death sentence unto itself. As a result of the diagnosis, she was planning to retire from her job immediately. While a guilty plea carries a mandatory six-month minimum sentence, the defendant's medical condition can qualify her for a suspended sentence, that is, if the judge exercises his discretionary powers and the indications are he will. This is the so-called get-out-of-jail card. As a condition of the deal, Staci Ballard must turn over her medical records to the court, verifying her condition."

Staci and Roland…bonded in the end by cruel fate, Adam thought.

Stevens clasped his hands upon the notes he was reading from and eyed his small audience. "There are still a few details to be worked out, but all in all, I consider this a fair plea deal. Any questions?"

Before he took any, he turned to Westwood. "I'm sorry your trip into the past ended like this, but I think you can take satisfaction justice was served."

"I do," Westwood replied with a trace of resignation. "Are you surprised Bob Ballard ended up accepting the deal?" he asked.

"A bit," he answered. "No doubt it was his wife who pressed him for a settlement. She indicated why when she requested copies of the sketches for her own keeping." The prosecutor looked to Ginny Perkins. "Okay with you?"

"Of course," she said.

"This case isn't going to make the headlines," Stevens

concluded, "and that may be best for all. The important thing is the record is being set straight, thanks in large measure to all of you."

With that, the prosecutor gathered up his notes and left, followed by Westwood who informed Adam on his way out he would drop by his office in the next day or two to settle the bill.

Adam looked to the woman across the table who had altered the course of the hearing. "You did good, Ginny. If you hadn't brought Kati back to life, all of this would have been for naught."

She said nothing, letting the appreciation in her eyes say it for her.

"Oh, by the way, may I call you Ginny, or do you prefer Aunt Ginny?"

She tilted her head and flashed him a smile. "You know," she said, more as a statement than a question.

"One of my last steps in the investigation was to make a quick side trip to the nursing home Paul Madden resided in before he passed away. I checked the log book for visitors, you know, for the same reason the major media outlets regularly check the White House log book to keep track of visitors in case a person of interest shows up. Anyway, I noticed an 'Aunt Ginny' entered in the visitor's log next to Paul Madden's name. It didn't take much figuring to conclude it was in fact you who was the aunt to Paul."

Ginny acknowledged the connection with a nod.

"Can you now tell me the rest of the story?" Adam asked politely.

"Yes, I was Paul's aunt. Still am in spirit, though I was not much older than he at the time. I had two sisters, the one I had mentioned in court killed in the war and an older one. He was my older sister's son. On my last visit to the nursing home shortly before his death, I brought along the sketches of Kati for him to see one last time. She was the love of his life and nothing I could have done would have pleased him more."

"When did he first see them?" Adam asked

"Not long after I had come to realize it was Kati I had sketched that day on the bridge. You must remember I had never seen her up until the incident. After what I felt was an appropriate time, I let him know how they came into existence."

"Why didn't you give them to him at the time?"

"A fair question and the answer helps explain how the impact of what occurred on the bridge lasted a lifetime for those involved and why it took a lifetime for the truth to surface. Paul Madden did not know his girlfriend had planned an outing on the bridge the day she was killed. Nor did he know Staci and Mr. Westwood were planning to be there. He first learned of the incident on his return from the short family vacation he had taken to the Keys."

"Did you speak with him about the incident?" Adam asked.

"No, I did not. At the time we were not that close. As I said on the witness stand, I lived quite a distance away, far enough to not hear the news Kati was killed in the incident."

"When did you come to learn of her death?"

"A month or two later when my sister, in a casual conversation, mentioned her son's girlfriend had been killed in a bridge incident. After I got off the phone, I realized it must have been the bridge incident I witnessed and Paul's girlfriend I had sketched."

"Did you mention it to anyone?"

"Not at the time. No one had interviewed me concerning the incident, nor did I have any reason to suspect there was foul play. My sister said it was an accident and I took it to be that. As I mentioned, after an appropriate time I let him know the sketches existed. It was not until Mr. Westwood came along after all these years, that I learned, like you, that the incident was something other than an accident. When I returned your call and the lady who answered the phone identified your firm as Adam Fraley Private Investigations, I instinctively knew it must have something to do with what happened on that bridge. That is why I brought along the sketches to our first meeting."

"Whatever became of Paul following Kati's death?"

"He was devastated. To try and get it all behind him, he joined the military, much like Mr. Westwood did. He served several years overseas in a number of different posts. It was during this period I came to know him better. My sister let it be known he welcomed letters from the home front, so I initiated a correspondence with him. When the war ended he returned home and became an over-the-road truck driver, a job he held until his retirement. He liked life on the road. The independent lifestyle gave him time to reflect, he said."

"You kept in touch with him?"

"Yes, we continued our pen-pal relationship that we'd started in the war. In his letters, he would describe for me the many changes of scenery he experienced over a long haul. I had never been out of the state of Florida and found his travel reports fascinating. He would also get introspective with me at times, telling me there would never be another Kati Carew in his life and because of it, he would never give up his wanderlust existence. Over the course of our letter writing, there actually came a time when Paul seemed to be of a mind he was corresponding directly with Kati. He often would refer to 'our' trips to the beach or 'our' walks in the park and how much he missed them. I suppose it was his way of living in the past. To some it might seem an unwise thing to do. Better to get on with life they might say, but it was his choice and an indication of his feelings toward her. He once told me he kept a photo of her pinned to his cab's sun visor, right next to his St. Christopher medal. One kept him safe, the other kept him warm, he said."

"There are those today who would call it nothing more or less than the usual high school romance," Adam opined.

"They would be wrong," Ginny said.

"How so?" Adam asked, struck by the firmness of her comeback. "You don't by chance have a sketch hidden away to illustrate the storied nature of it, do you?" he jested

"Much has happened to push back the past, Adam, but I still have the evidence it was something other than the usual teen romance."

"Letters tucked away in shoe boxes?"

"Letters tucked away here," she said tapping her temple.

She paused before continuing. "I know he made a point of visiting her grave site whenever he returned from a long, over-the-road trip. His truck had become his home and remained so until old age caught up with him. In the end, when he was no longer able to meet the physical demands of the job, he retired and soon after placed himself in a nursing home. Yet, he continued as long as he could his visits to her grave," she said, resurrecting in Adam's mind the image of the withered floral bouquet resting at the foot of her tombstone.

"He died not knowing how Kati actually died," Adam observed.

"It was probably best he didn't know," she said

"Did he ever mention Staci in his letters?"

"Never, until the end," she said. "It has to do with your earlier question of why I didn't give him the sketches. I did, in fact, offer them to him at our final meeting but he declined the offer, saying he already had them embedded in his mind. 'Give them to Staci,' he said, which I was about to do until you came along. It goes without saying that if I had given them to her, the course of events might have taken a different turn."

"How long of an interim do you estimate between the time you intended to give them to Staci and the moment I came on the scene?" he dared to ask.

She held up her thumb and forefinger and spread them about a half inch apart. "About that long," she said.

"The truth always has a way of coming out, no matter the time and circumstance," Adam said. "But that's cutting it pretty close."

Ginny reached down beside her chair to retrieve her ever-present sketch folder. Fingering through it, she slipped out another sketch and handed it to Adam who, upon viewing it, was at once bemused and flattered. "You've got me looking very happy," he said.

"You have a killer smile, Adam," she said with a sparkle in her eye.

"In the business I'm in, the term 'killer' usually takes on a whole different meaning."

"I'm sure the ladies know what I mean."

"Well, I do have a date tonight. I'll have to keep that in mind."

She nodded her approval.

"Do you have a ride home?" he asked.

"I came in a cab and I'm leaving in a cab," she said.

"Forget it, I'm giving you a ride home."

CHAPTER THIRTEEN

"Why are you smiling?" Tamra asked, searching his face for clues.

"Someone wise to the ways of the world told me I should be doing more of it."

"Is your former boss still serving as your personal and professional mentor? That doesn't sound like something he would advise."

"Pete Peterson's still a mentor of mine and will continue to be, but it wasn't he who advised it. What Pete did offer advice on was the propriety of my asking you out."

Adam chose Orologio's Restaurant, a favorite of both, for the dinner date. Its many nooks and crannies, relaxed atmosphere, and reliably delicious Italian cuisine made it ideal for those who wanted to keep their dining experience casual and private.

"I'll assume he saw no impropriety in it," she said with a soft smile.

She wore a clinging, copper-colored satin dress that matched the auburn hair she had loosened to the shoulders. Even her lipstick had a moistened, copper-hued tone. Gone were the reading glasses she wore at work, along with her proper corporate demeanor. In short, she looked gorgeous, dangerously gorgeous, not to mention relaxed and confident, all of which greatly contributed to Adam's nervousness. He realized immediately he was looking at her in a completely different light.

"Pete is not big on propriety. On the contrary, he was encouraging. He said I would be displaying no favoritism, since there was no one else around to favor. Of course, large companies frown on it for a number of reasons, the primary one being if it doesn't work out, the aftermath can be messy and oftentimes cause widespread and irreparable collateral damage to the company. Who knows, the same could hold true for the small business as well."

Tamra's smile widened. "Are you having second thoughts?" she asked.

Realizing the inappropriateness of his remarks, Adam looked across to her with as much seriousness as he could muster. "You know, what I just said about collateral damage, forget it," he insisted. "Right about now, if you took that glass of wine in your hand and threw it in my face, no one would blame you, including me."

Tamra raised her wine glass. "Why waste a good glass of wine," she said. "Better we push the restart button."

Adam raised his in kind. "Restart it will be."

"The preliminary trial did not go as expected?" she asked.

"Somewhat. The sketches were devastating for the defense, legally and emotionally. If Bob Ballard had had his way, the contest might have continued on. Staci, according to Stevens, would have none of it," Adam explained. "As things stand I do have a meeting scheduled with the prosecutor tomorrow afternoon to tie up a loose end."

"There's more to the story?" she asked.

"Nothing worth discussing now," Adam said. "Enough of the shop talk, anyway. The trial is over and the verdict cast. That's it."

"So sad in so many ways, yet a win is a win," she said.

"The question now is, what is the chance of a win in Noelle's upcoming playoff game?" he asked, sinking his fork into his pasta dish.

Tamra laid down her fork. "I'll be honest, Adam," she said. "There's about as much chance of a plate of pasta not being served in this place tonight as there is of Noelle's Southside Pirates serving up a win."

Adam's gaze fell on the two pasta dishes having been served them. "My God, we're already doomed!"

Tamra chuckled. "Maybe I was overly pessimistic. Remember what the sports prognosticators say whenever a mismatch appears in the making. That's why they play the game."

Adam took a sip of wine, contemplating the challenge awaiting his daughter. "I'm concerned for her," he said, adopting a parental tone. "Whether it's her school work or athletic endeavors, she throws herself fully into them. She's overly competitive, which I know comes as no great revelation to you."

"What's wrong with that? We live in a competitive society."

"Nothing's wrong with it, as long as you're prepared to bear the losing side of it. I'm not sure she is. She's been practicing her swing non-stop. Too bad there's not a practice routine for losing."

"You're a worrier, Adam. You have the responsibility of a parent. Naturally, you're going to worry. It's a sign you accept the responsibility of being one. However, you don't want to let your worrying become a detriment to your long-term health."

He suppressed a laugh. "I worry about those who don't worry, so I worry for them."

"Unfortunately, learning to lose gracefully comes with losing. Still, this could turn out to be a teaching lesson for her. The truth is success can be found in failure. It happens in all aspects of life, whether it's athletics, school work, or personal relationships."

Relationships, the romantic kind in which he was presently engaged, were beginning to invite comparisons. Tamra and Carlita were both intelligent, attractive, confident, and engaging women. In fact, they had more in common than not. Sure, Tamra was a bit edgier, but the major feature separating the two was that Tamra was here and Carlita there, a half continent away. It all begged the question, why not leave the choice up to Noelle? After all, who else had a better handle on all the parties involved? Who else would be more impacted? Who else had an opinion on the matter that carries more weight? The answer to all, of course, was he, Adam. Other men would view his present predicament as an embarrassment of riches, would they not? Then why was he playing the role of the great procrastinator? At the root of his indecision, he decided, was the question of which came first, the desire to marry or love? The answer, he learned from a lifetime of observing, was not so simple.

"You look to be in deep thought," Tamra said, twirling a portion of pasta on her fork and spoon.

"What kind of a man are you looking for?" he asked outright, immediately wishing he hadn't.

"Who said I was looking?" came the appropriate reply.

"Strike two," he thought. "Maybe I should let you ask the next question," he said, fearing a third.

"Okay, I'll bite," she said, laying her fork and spoon aside. "What do you consider the worst reason for getting married, the one that guarantees a bad outcome?"

"I have to narrow it down to one?" he asked, taking a bite out of a bread stick.

She nodded, her mouth busy with a mouthful of pasta.

"Do you have a specific answer in mind?" he asked.

"I do, but rather than guess my answer, give me your own."

"Wouldn't it be better if mine matched yours."

"It would help."

"Help with what?"

"With the evening," she said, straightforwardly.

"Here comes the third strike," he thought. "Okay, here goes, time is running out, worst reason to get married. That's my answer and I'm sticking to it," he said, raising his wine glass to toast his response.

A smile slowly creased her face. "Very good. You must be reading the same magazines I've been reading."

That was another quality he admired in a woman, the ability to make a man feel comfortable in their presence no matter the circumstance, particularly this one. His comfort level was approaching hers, due to no great effort on his part.

"There's a big plus in courting a co-worker," his former boss had once advised him. "Put simply, you both come pre-approved. Yep, you're already beyond that chemistry-on-the-first-date crap. Whether you realize it or not, you've got a head start into determining the long-term potential of a possible mate. That's not to say desire doesn't enter into the picture," he'd went on. "Look at desire as a latent thing, ready to be reawakened at the appropriate time, like the second date."

All well and good, Adam reckoned, but for the remainder of the evening, there was no way he could turn a blind eye to the beauty sitting across from him. The fact was, he was blissfully caught in the chemistry of the first date and had no way, much less desire, of escaping it. No, he was more inclined to pretend she was someone other than his office manager and thereby dismiss out of hand all the built-in restrictions that accompany a professional relationship. But, alas, he came to realize there was no way of separating the professional from the personal. Yet, on second thought, wasn't it the totality of the package that made it at once intoxicating and sobering?

———

"All things considered, did the evening go as expected?" he asked himself before retiring to bed at the end of the evening. "Better than expected," he opined, thanks to a last-minute bit of advice from his daughter.

"Did you find a babysitter for Noelle?" Tamra had asked at her condo doorstep at the close of the date.

"She's reached the age where she feels she no longer needs one, so I went along with her wish," he said. "I did alert a neighbor woman who said she would periodically check on her."

"She needs to get her rest and not worry about the upcoming game, or else I'd invite you in for a nightcap," she replied.

"I told her she'd better be in bed by the time I arrived home," he said in response to her concern. "Oh, by the way, she did issue me her own last-minute command before I left," he quickly added.

He recalled Tamra cocking her head at the remark, as an uncertain smile formed slowly on her face.

"I can hear her now if I ignore it," he recalled saying to her. "Oh, brother, don't tell me you didn't."

"Didn't do what?" Tamra had responded, her interest tweaked.

At that point Adam had reached out and taken her by the hand, carefully tracking her eyes to see if she averted his at the moment of his touch. Excepting an incidental brush of her hand or shoulder during the course of the workday, he had never before touched her in such a personal manner. Any averting of eyes on her part and he would have scrubbed his next move. Fortunately, she didn't, keeping them locked on his as he drew her closer. Her scent, as intoxicating as anything wafting from a Frangipani tree, overcame whatever reluctance he had left. An instant later, he was lost in a kiss, in the warmth and ease of her embrace, in the gentle press of her hand against the back of his neck, in the commingling of genuine affection and guilty pleasure for which he had no defense, if indeed, it was a defense he was in want of.

Perhaps it was best she didn't invite him in, he had convinced himself on the walk back to his car. Amid the wave of reflection, one burning realization overwhelmed all others. On this night he had kissed his office manager.

"Let the lawsuits fly," he was of a mind to shout, despite the wackiness of the thought. Ending his recollection of the evening from the comfort of his bed, he knew one thing was for certain. Employee relations at Adam Fraley Private Investigations would never again be the same.

CHAPTER FOURTEEN

BETTY ANN CARVER'S HOME WAS A WELL-KEPT BUNGALOW strung between other bungalows in a sprawling middle class-section of St. Petersburg. On entering, Adam discovered that the interior of the home was no less immaculate and ordered than the exterior, so much so he felt it necessary to limit his movements lest he become the bull in the china shop. At her invitation he settled into a cushy armchair across from where she sat on small divan. She was wearing a polka-dot blue and white smock and a permanent smile on her chubby face.

"Would you care for a cup of coffee?" she asked.

"No, thank you."

"I must say, I was surprised to hear from you, especially after Roland Westwood came calling on the same matter not so long ago," she said in a hearty voice that belied her petite stature and age. "Are you also searching for Staci Carew?"

"No, Staci's been found."

"Oh, where?"

"She's married and living in Tampa."

"Such a terrible thing, losing her sister like that," she said, shaking her head. "I suppose you know all about it."

"Yes, Roland filled me in the circumstances surrounding her death."

"You mentioned on the phone you were interested in finding information on the general store run by the family. What in particular may I ask?"

"I understand there was a robbery at the store shortly after Kati Carew's death."

"There sure was and it couldn't have occurred at a worse time. The Carew family was already dealing with one tragic situation when they were handed another right on the heels of it, of far less importance, of course."

"Can you give me some details about the robbery?" he asked.

"Is that thing still being investigated?" she asked in bewilderment. "I've heard of cold cases but that would take the cake."

"No, not officially. It's being looked at in light of the Kati Carew tragedy and its effect on the family, coming at the inopportune time it did," Adam explained.

"Well, the robbery turned out to be a total mystery, for sure. We ended up with five thousand dollars missing and no explanation for how it disappeared."

"No idea of who might have run off with it?"

"No, none whatsoever. There was no sign of forced entry, nor was there anything else taken at the time."

"An overnight heist?"

"Apparently, and the only major one to occur at the store in its entire existence. We were located in an area where crime was as rare as freezing temperatures. There was some talk of maybe a tourist or drifter passing through committing the theft, but like I said, there was no sign of forced entry, or any other evidence, for that matter."

"You were the assistant manager?"

"Yes, on a part time basis. I also was attending college. Mr. and Mrs. Carew pretty much operated the store themselves. It was hard work, running it from seven in the morning to seven in the evening, Monday through Saturday."

"Did their girls put in any time working there?"

"No, the parents wanted them to concentrate on their school work. They did pick up some spending money doing occasional babysitting jobs, from what I understand."

"How about their summers?"

"The parents also believed in seeing to it their summers were free, so they could fully enjoy their teenage years. There was one thing they especially made clear. They did not want them to feel an obligation to carry on the family business. That was another reason they did not wish to put them on the store payroll. They wanted them to pursue their own interests."

"And those were?"

"For Kati it was gymnastics. For Staci I'm not sure. Chasing boys would be my guess," she said through one of her hearty laughs. "Or maybe I should say having them chase her."

"Who kept track of the money at the store?"

"Mr. Carew and I."

"It was kept in a safe?"

She laughed. "In a locked drawer. Remember, this was a more innocent time."

"Was that an unusually large amount of cash on hand?"

"Not unusual, but when it came close to five thousand, we would see to it that a bank deposit was made."

"Who would have known there was five thousand dollars in the drawer?"

"Any one of us. Believe me, from the beginning I knew I would be under the microscope by the investigators, since it looked like it might have been an inside job. Fortunately, I was out of town visiting friends the night the money disappeared, so I was cleared immediately."

"Do you remember who conducted the investigation?"

"The sheriff's department."

"Do you recall by chance the name of the lead investigator?"

"I sure do...Glen Martin. He was a regular customer of the store."

"Did either Mr. or Mrs. Carew have an opinion of him?"

"They seemed to get along fine."

"The case was never solved?"

"Like I said, there was no evidence, no fingerprints other than those of people who worked there, no witnesses, no nothing."

"What was the name of the store?"

"The General Store. Creative, huh?"

"You said the Carew girls did not work there. Did they hang out there much?"

"They dropped in occasionally."

"Together or separately?"

"Separately, most of the time. Kati usually would come in alone. Her sister always had a group of friends tagging along with her. The store served as a favorite gathering spot for the locals, both kids and adults, to do their gossiping or whatever. There wasn't much else around."

"Lots of foot traffic?"

"Lots. Business was good."

"Whatever became of the store?"

"It's now an antique shop, specializing in Floridiana. Doing well from what I hear."

The conversation soon slipped into small talk, leading Adam to diplomatically cut the visit short, citing an appointment up in Pasco County he had to make.

"Be sure and say hello to Roland and Staci," Betty Ann said, escorting him to the door.

———

"Okay, let's hear the loose end you got," Stevens said, scooting his black leather chair back from his elongated mahogany desk to stretch his legs.

Adam related the story of the Carew family general store and in particular the coincidence of the overall heist coming close on the heels of the Kati Carew tragedy. "You have to admit, the sheriff's report on Kati's death comes across as a halfhearted effort, if not outright sloppy," he said. "There was no verification of Staci's and Westwood's whereabouts on the day of the accident, no checking of tire tracks to determine what cars might have been there. No effort to check if fingerprints were present anywhere on the bridge, no checking for footprints, no thought given to searching Kati's old lockers, no awareness of a nudist camp located approximate to the bridge. For the most part, they took everyone's word on what occurred at face value, including the medical examiner's."

"And you're thinking this all deliberate?" Stevens said, clasping his hands atop his head.

"If five thousand bucks was taken and there were no signs of forced entry, it sure looks like it was an inside job. The assistant manager had a solid alibi. That leaves the parents. Why would they filch it when apparently, they didn't need it? The store did a good business, according to the assistant manager. And how coincidental was it that Glen Martin also headed up the robbery investigation? Yes, I know there was a severe wartime personnel shortage, but it all seems much too convenient in hindsight."

Stevens released his hands from atop his head and clasped them in his lap. "Are you suggesting there was extortion of some sort at play?"

"Not necessarily. More like someone doing someone a special favor. Martin was a regular patron of the store, after all. He would be doing the community a big favor as well, wrapping up the case quickly so the healing could begin."

"And he was rewarded monetarily for his efforts. Is that what you're saying?" Stevens asked skeptically.

"The five thousand went for something," Adam said. "It's not totally unreasonable to think there was a connection between the theft and the bridge incident."

Stevens scooted his chair closer to the desk, resting his arms on top of it. "Look, Adam, there are hurdles to be cleared before the D. A.'s office considers bringing a charge against an individual. Before you say it, I know there were significant hurdles in the Kati Carew case, but what you are suggesting poses even greater obstacles. First of all, there are no eyewitnesses like there were in the bridge incident to what you are suggesting. Secondly, there is no hard evidence to what you are intimating. Third, there are reasons for statutes of limitation."

"For co-conspirators in a felony offense?"

"Okay, granted, you may have a point there." Stevens said. "However, what you're suggesting is pure conjecture and this office doesn't base its decisions on guesswork."

"What about Glen Martin?"

"What about him?"

"An interview with him might clear things up."

"You wouldn't be thinking of a bug, would you now?"

"Say, there's an idea," Adam quipped.

"Before you go down that path, I should tell you we looked into Martin's past as part of our preparation for the Kati Carew trial and it turned out his record was clean. That's not to say he didn't screw up the investigation. Maybe he did rush things as a favor to a friend. For sure, the preliminary trial laid bare its deficiencies. Does that mean we go after Martin? I'm afraid I disagree with you on that point, even though I do agree there may be a hint of truth in what you say."

Stevens straightened his chair. "Here is my view in hindsight, nothing of which can be proved. If I took what I'm about to say to any other D. A's office in the state, there's a good chance he or she would laugh me out of the room. Remember, thinking it and proving it are two entirely different thought patterns in the eyes of a prosecutor. As part of our job, we are constantly weighing the pros and cons of filing charges, mostly based on the hard evidence at hand. It is a highly selective process, believe me." Stevens paused before proceeding. "Do you have children, Adam?" he asked.

"Yes, I have a daughter."

"As you undoubtedly know, parents will go to extraordinary lengths to protect their children, even from the arms of the law, and even if they are aware of their guilt. It happens all the time. Rather than Martin extorting or pressing Kati's parents for money to skewer the sheriff's report, I believe it more likely the Carew parents, having somehow gotten word of Staci's presence on the bridge, perhaps from Staci herself, decided to take the initiative and offer the five thousand on hand to Martin to distort the report. Whether the money actually passed hands, we have no way of proving. The bank records have long since been expunged. Perhaps, and I emphasize perhaps, Martin did it as a favor...*pro bono*...if you will, but to go after him now is a fool's errand. What is there to gain? His report has been discredited and, in the end, Kati got her justice as a result. Don't turn victory into defeat. Believe me, there are always loose ends to a case, very few of them worth chasing once the main issue is settled. Besides, the loose end in this case is, or should I say was, ours to tackle, not yours."

A brief silence ensued between the two.

"Why are you grinning?" Stevens asked.

"I was speaking with a former boss of mine about this before I came over. He serves as my unofficial mentor. His response was much the same as yours. 'You go chasing too many loose ends, you end up chasing your own tail,' he said. He not so subtly reminded me I have a business to run, something my office manager continually brings to my attention."

"There you go. You now have a second and third opinion. As I said, mark this one up as a win. You have fulfilled your client's reason for hire, have you not?"

"Yes, I believe I have."

"Well then, time for you to move on to your next case. This one's over."

Adam nodded his agreement. Satisfied his assignment was complete, he headed home.

CHAPTER FIFTEEN

SOMEONE THREW A BLOCK PARTY FOR THE COMMUNITY surrounding Parker Field and decided to hold it in the stadium itself, or so it appeared at first sight to Adam. A raucous crowd filled the sun-bathed ballpark, no doubt lured by the growing celebrity status of the North Bay Sharks' pitcher Rita Brownback.

The contest started on a positive note. Someone other than Harlan Weeks was calling balls and strikes behind the plate. Conceivably, the league had come to its senses after all, Adam concluded.

From the outset Brownback did not disappoint her fans, overpowering Southside Pirates' hitters with her perfected rise ball, occasionally mixing in a drop ball to further frustrate the batters. Through five innings the southpaw phenom had fanned twelve hitters, giving up no hits and no runs. Noelle fared no better than the rest of her teammates, striking out twice and looking hapless in both plate appearances. Yet, the vintage wooden scoreboard rising above the center field fence let everyone know it was still a tied ball game heading into the sixth inning. The Pirate hurler had also managed to hold the Sharks without a run, thanks to some clutch pitching on her part and a stellar defensive effort by her teammates that included two double plays. What the Pirates couldn't afford to do at this stage of the contest was let their opponent grab any kind of a lead with Brownback on the mound

That's exactly what happened in a disastrous top of the sixth for the Pirates. The Sharks had the go-ahead run on second base following a two-out double. The next hitter dribbled a weak ground ball off the end of her bat down the first base line where Noelle Fraley was positioned. Normally, a sure-handed fielder, Noelle made the fundamental mistake of lifting her head before the ball was in her glove. Consequently, it squirted through her legs and into right field, allowing the runner to scramble home from second with the lead run. The North Bay fans across the way erupted in cheers, as Noelle lowered her hands to her knees and her head toward the ground in dejection. The Pirate pitcher retired the next hitter on a pop-up for the third out, but the damage had already been done.

Adam watched with despair as his daughter jogged back to the bench to face her cohorts. To let your teammates down was the worst of the worst for a player. Oh, how he wanted to run out on the field and console her. He now understood why some parents chose not to sit in the stands to watch their children compete in high-pressure games.

"It's not over yet," Tamra said with little conviction from her seat beside him.

"If only it was," he said to himself.

Brownback sailed through the bottom of the sixth with ease, registering two more strikeouts while preserving her no-hitter. Unable to build on their lead in the top of the seventh, the Sharks headed into the bottom of the inning still clinging to their one-run lead. As far as Adam was concerned, it might as well be a ten-run lead with Brownback on the mound.

The large contingent of North Bay fans were on their feet as their ace pitcher took to the mound, stamping their feet with such force it reverberated across the grandstand to where Adam and Tamra sat with solemn faces along with the other Southside faithful.

Noelle was slated to be the fifth hitter up for the Pirates in the bottom of the seventh, their final at bat, making it highly unlikely she would have another turn at the plate. A mixed blessing, Adam reckoned.

Brownback appeared to be losing nothing off her rise ball, beginning the inning much the same way she had the previous six with two strikeouts, stirring the crowd into a fever pitch, as the prospect of a perfect game loomed large. The "Backbreaker" appeared to have mercifully ended the contest when the third batter swung at a two-strike pitch and missed. However, the North Bay catcher found Brownback's pitches nearly as difficult to catch as to hit, letting the third strike carom off her glove back to the backstop. The passed ball allowed the hitter to reach first, thereby spoiling the perfect game, if not the no-hitter. A moment later Brownback made her first mistake, plunking the next hitter in the back with a pitch that got away from her, putting runners on first and second with two outs. The North Bay coach immediately trotted to the mound to consult with her star pitcher.

"No way is she going to yank her," Adam said aloud.

"She's just settling her down," Tamra replied. "It's not like Brownback is used to having runners on the bases with the game on the line."

Meanwhile, striding toward the plate for the Pirates was Noelle. She had yet to reach the batter's box before the Southside coach jogged out to speak to her.

"Oh, no, I hope he's not going to pull her for a pinch hitter," Tamra lamented.

The idea of a pinch hitter was not one Adam easily dismissed. "Perhaps it would be best," the man of little faith ruminated.

The two coaches trotted back to their respective benches, leaving matters to pitcher and hitter.

It was southpaw versus southpaw, making the task doubly difficult for Noelle. The pause in play while the coaches were giving their final instructions allowed the Sharks' fans to rev up the crowd again. Once more, the stands reverberated from the stamping of feet and chorus of strident voices.

Noelle stood in the batter's box, her bat leveled behind her left shoulder, her eyes peering over her right at Brownback. She took the first pitch for a strike, the ball exploding over the outside corner of the plate like a cannon shot. There was no doubt the 'Backbreaker' was back to form following a momentary lapse. The second delivery Noelle fouled back, running the count to 0-2. She was down to her last strike. The third pitch barely rose above the strike zone, as did the fourth, evening the count and prolonging Adam's agony. The fifth pitch clearly was outside the strike zone, running the count full. Noelle fought off the next two pitches, tapping one off to the side of the plate and fouling the other back to the backstop.

"She's getting her timing right," Tamra said from aside him. "She just needs to get the head of the bat flush on the ball."

The fans were in full uproar. If there had been a roof over their heads, it would have long since been raised to the heavens.

Brownback went into her windmill windup and let fly her next pitch. Noelle swung and missed, sending the North Bay crowd into a frenzy, or did she? The plate umpire was frantically swiping his hands, signaling something other.

"Foul tip!" Tamra said with raised voice. "The catcher couldn't hold on to it."

Given new life, Noelle again stepped to the plate and took her stance, this time edging as close to the front of the batter's box as she could without stepping out of it.

Everyone in the stadium was now on their feet, including Adam and Tamra. Amid the delirium North Bay fans struck up a chant "Strikeout! Strikeout! Strikeout!"

"I hope she doesn't decide to throw her a drop ball," Adam said. "It will freeze her."

"Noelle knows she isn't," Tamra said confidently. "She's going to stick with the pitch that got her here."

Brownback toed the rubber, checked the runners, and launched into her windmill windup, unleashing the pitch she had perfected, the dreaded rise ball.

And then it happened. Cutting through the roar of the crowd

came the sound unheard for the entirety of the game, the clank of a metal bat meeting a ball dead center, sending it on a line over the outstretched glove of the shortstop toward the gap between the left and center fielders, neither of whom was able to cut if off from its path to the fence.

Like many in the crowd, Adam at first looked on in stunned silence, but not Tamra who was screaming her lungs out in delight.

The runners scurried around the bases, the third base coach frantically waving them home, first the tying run followed by the winning one.

Noelle stood on second base, her arms stretched skyward in triumph, as teammates and fans rushed the field to congratulate her. As they raised her on their shoulders, she looked into the stands to her two biggest fans who were saluting her with repeated fist pumps. It was at that moment, amid the wild celebration, Adam noticed Rita Brownback halting her slow walk from the mound to try and catch the attention of Noelle. Patiently, she waited, surrounded by a sea of happy faces, until Noelle noticed her in the middle of the hubbub, at which point Brownback extended her arm and gave her a thumbs-up.

Rita Brownback may have been a loser this day, Adam thought, but she was a winner in life, a lesson he hoped would not be lost on Noelle.

As he watched the scene unfold before them, with his daughter riding the shoulders of her teammates, Adam could not help but be reminded of another time and place long ago when a young girl stood with her arms raised in triumph, a time when first loves were forever, summers endless, and young lives full of promise; of a bridge over the Withlacoochee River and Kati Carew, the backflip girl, whose summer of life was never to be.

Oh, Staci...if only it had been a thumbs-up you had given your sister.

Unwilling to finish the thought, Adam found himself fighting off a bout of melancholy like Noelle fought off those pitches.

"Ready to go give you daughter a hug," Tamra said from his side in the wake of the victory.

"Couldn't be more ready," he said, leaving the past and the melancholy behind.

THE END

Don't miss out on your next favorite book!

Join the Melange Books mailing list at
www.melange-books.com/mail.html

THANK YOU FOR READING

Did you enjoy this book?

We invite you to leave a review at the website of your choice, such as Goodreads, Amazon, Barnes & Noble, etc.

DID YOU KNOW THAT LEAVING A REVIEW...

- Helps other readers find books they may enjoy.
- Gives you a chance to let your voice be heard.
- Gives authors recognition for their hard work.
- Doesn't have to be long. A sentence or two about why you liked the book will do.

ABOUT THE AUTHOR

Henry Hoffman is a former newspaper editor and public library director whose works have appeared in a variety of literary and trade publications, including the Library Journal, the Midwesterner, Encyclopedia of Library Science, America: History and Life, Historical Abstracts of the United States, the Cyclopedia of Literary Places, and the Encyclopedia of Natural Disasters. He is the author of five previous novels, including Bridge to Oblivion and The Veiled Lagoon, the first two entries in the Adam Fraley mystery series. He is the recipient of the Florida Publishers Association's Gold Medal Award for Florida Fiction.

www.henryhoffman.net

ALSO BY HENRY HOFFMAN

WITH MELANGE BOOKS

Adam Fraley Mysteries

On A Midnight Clear

The Ephemeral File

www.ingramcontent.com/pod-product-compliance
Lightning Source LLC
Chambersburg PA
CBHW020613250626
47154CB00004B/1494